A

Billet-doux

From the Heart

Cheryl Jennings

Published by:
Cheryl Jennings & SokheChapke Publishing
Copyright ©2024
SokheChapke Publishing, Inc.

Library of Congress Cataloging-in publication data
ISBN: 9798895901113

Published and printed in the United States of
America. Jennings, Cheryl
A Billet-doux From the Heart by Cheryl Jennings

Dedicated......

to anyone who has experienced the pleasure or the painful sting of love... and its unimagined consequences.

PART ONE

PART TWO

PART THREE

A Billet-doux From The Heart

PART ONE

Chapter 1
Encounter

Engineer Eric Blake was handsome. He was so jaw-dropping that describing his mesmerizing appeal was inexplicably beyond anyone's comprehension. His noticeably slow and easy swagger was a provocative force that most women couldn't help but notice. He was, in the best way, every woman's self-indulgent daydream.

One afternoon, in San Honesto, captivated onlookers watched Eric leave Garcia's Restaurant near the University of Scientific Technology (UST). The trendy Mexican neighborhood staple was packed with hungry lunchgoers waiting to be seated, while lingering, satisfied diners casually sipped ice-filled drinks.

Despite the heat rising from several shamelessly self-abandoned admirers, Eric ignored their longing glances. But when he took a short path back to his office, a stunning, brown-skinned woman with wavy, coal-black hair instantly ambushed his attention. Right away, the engineer rushed across the parking lot, hoping to take in more of her alluring enchantment. The mysteriously fascinating woman had dealt him an urgent mission in an unexpected twist of fate.

Triggered by an impulse, he walked faster because he didn't want to lose sight of her in the crowded plaza. Casual shoppers crossed his path, yet nothing stopped his pursuit. He was determined to introduce himself before she vanished. Ignoring caution, Eric darted between speeding cars and came within inches of being struck by a speeding red convertible. Another enraged motorist at the disruptive scene stomped his SUV's brakes and laid on the car's horn for nearly a minute. The frustrated driver in the convertible yelled a string of obscenities and waved her middle finger at the well-heeled, traffic-jamming pedestrian, who never looked back at her. As Eric continued the pursuit, the noisy chaos piqued motorists, who eventually moved on.

The vehicular frenzy didn't bother Olivia Reece, who searched her car for documents that needed an immediate postmark. It would have been easier to send the packet electronically, but the European recipients required a guarantee of university-authorized, original hard-copy files by the following week. In such a case, she had to trust the express air mail service to deliver it on time. Meanwhile, the Post Office was getting crowded as she watched several people entering the tiny storefront. It had not been her plan to stand in a long line to mail the documents, but then, she had no choice. To make matters worse, she was about to be late for her afternoon class.

"Damn! I guess it's at home," said she.

Although the San Honesto Post Office was filled with students, UST Professor Reece had to get back to campus within the hour to teach a course on quantum theory.

In one last attempt to find the missing packet, Olivia looked inside the physics textbook on the back seat and found it wedged between two dog-eared pages. All the while, she was unaware that Eric Blake had eventually reached her.

"Hello." From sensuously curved lips came a warm, radiant smile.

Olivia's eyes touched a man with the most pleasing

caramel skin, compelling dark eyes, and a seductive, irresistible aura. Everything about him was intensely appealing. Eric's unheralded approach swirled around her like an abrupt wind in the sultry heat; she couldn't have brushed him aside, even if she tried.

"May I get the door for you?" He paused as she eased out of the car. "I'm Eric Blake," he continued while stumbling over words that appeared to be straight from a college playboy's playbook. By that time, he had forgotten most of what he intended to say. "I was thinking... well...thinking you might need some assistance. May I carry a package for you if you're going into the Post Office?"

Olivia couldn't put her finger on it, but his sudden interlope into her tightly sealed orbit caught her interest by surprise.

"It is nice to meet you, Eric. I'm Olivia Reece."

"Nice meeting you, too," he replied. He never broke his gaze from what struck him as the most beautiful face he'd ever seen.

Touched by his chivalry, she looked away from him, doing whatever she could to avoid his boyish attempts to get her attention. Speechless seconds went by, and Olivia spoke again. "I'd love to talk... but you know, Eric, the line in the Post Office is getting longer, and I have a class that starts in two hours. I'm so sorry," she confided while pointing toward the lobby crammed with young people.

"Are you a student at UST?"

She drew a slow, deep breath and stepped backward to remove herself from his potent influence, but the car door foiled her attempted getaway.

"No, I'm not. I teach Physics there. My class starts at

three o'clock."

With brows narrowed, Eric considered what that meant. Still smiling politely, he said, "Hello, Professor."

She imagined a perfect physique inside the stiffly starched white shirt complemented with a blue silk tie. This impeccably dressed man wore polished black leather shoes that forced a slight bend above the cuffs on neatly pressed, razor-creased slacks. No one could deny that he was the sweetest eye candy for the most playful female observers. In that innocently unscripted instance, nothing else mattered. Undeniably, the captivating professor had blown him away.

His eyes briefly roamed the car-filled area, now looking for more persuasive lines to keep her there. He was at a loss for words. But his confident style coaxed Olivia to linger; she, too, wasn't ready for the conversation to end. Eric's aggressive approach had evoked a pleasant intrigue. Almost always self-assured, she rarely lost composure, but in some way, this man was causing her to lose poise, and regaining self-control seemed hopeless.

Now flirting, Olivia said, "Gotta go, Eric. Meeting you is great, but I don't like being late for my students."

He wanted to reply cleverly but fixated on her drop-dead scarlet lips, which pouted when she spoke. And although cautious of the handsome aggressor, his cute, awkward flattery interested her all the more.

"If I promise to be prompt, would you go out with me? Maybe you can lecture me on the principles of being on time," he playfully begged.

"Don't know, maybe I will." She reacted to his teenage pick-up line light-heartedly. Once more, she attempted to move around him, hoping to reach the entrance before more people entered the building.

He pleaded for a second time. "What if I throw in a candlelight dinner for two? Will you go out with me then?"

At that point, resisting his charm was impossible. "What! Are you serious? You're telling me that dinner didn't come with the first offer you put out there?"

Together, they laughed, causing wariness to disappear. For a few seconds longer, there was hesitant silence and the anticipation of what might be said next hung in the air. Olivia inhaled, let go of a steady stream of air, and reminded Eric of needing to mail the envelope. To underscore the seriousness of her claim, she blithely waved the large brown mailer in his direction.

"Okay, Professor." Disappointed that she wanted to leave, he pleaded again, "Do we have a date... and if you say yes, how soon?" His words begged her to give in to his proposal. By now, the sexy, uninhibited tension between them was rising. Her smiling eyes danced across his tall frame while feeling very good about the chance encounter.

"Yes, I think I'd like that," she said in response.

Evidently pleased with meeting him, she offered her phone number, which he punched into his cell phone. In turn, he pressed his business card into her hand.

"Every number you'll ever need to reach me is on this card." His eyes were full of unreserved hope as he leaned closer to her.

Professor Reece was trying to get the envelope mailed despite meeting him. Her goal was to beat the crowd and get back to campus. She turned and walked toward the Post Office entrance, determined not to look back at the attractive man she'd just met.

Walking backward toward the row of storefronts where the United States flag furled gently in a twist of summer wind, Eric yelled, "Don't forget our date!"

From the very start, Olivia apprehended him, and Eric couldn't dismiss the hauntingly beautiful images of her. Throughout the afternoon, the thought of meeting her was a pleasant diversion from a mountain of paperwork on his desk. He wanted to see her again.

Around 6:00 P. M., on the same day, Dr. Reece prepared to leave campus after a spirited session with a class of fifty students. The three o'clock class had ended early and her grad assistant joined the students' hurried exodus. While storing a laptop, she missed an incoming call from Zane Adams. His voicemail invited her to a symposium at Eastern California University, so she took a few extra minutes to note the details, including a request to discuss findings related to the Krausberg Effect: a study of communication links from space, including methods for developing encryption keys.

In years of research, Reece discovered unpublished facts that satellites with weak encryptions presented security risks worldwide. Further study revealed Physicist Wolfgang Krausberg's theory on using encryption keys to protect satellite transmissions from nefarious adversaries. Since the U.S. dominated in this arena, she believed Krausberg's groundbreaking study and eventual findings would have a significant impact on global communication.

Olivia woke early the following morning in a pitch-black bedroom. She was restless, and the air conditioner was churning noisily on overdrive as it worked to ward off the summer heat in the valley. Along with frequent flashes of unbearable heatwaves, she was used to the wide-ranging, nature-inspired conditions in California, such as extreme temperatures, pop-up forest fires, and occasionally destructive earthquakes. These spectacular features, including beautiful beaches and hundreds of vineyards, created a fascinating playground for natives and tourists alike. She loved both the good and the bad of the Golden State; after all, it was her home.

"Eric, huh?" In the dark, she whispered his name, shut her eyes, and put her thoughts on the faculty meeting that would start hours later in the Dean's conference room. Although much younger than her fellow faculty, Olivia's colleagues welcomed her as a third-year Full Professor. Graduating with honors from a highly praised East Coast university had helped her land the coveted position at UST, an elite, private institution. In the role of teacher and researcher, she had found her true métier.

"The Dean will have a long agenda: Fall semester teaching assignments, blah, blah, blah," she mused. Her restlessness subsided after finding a comfortable spot in her pillow-soft bed. She soon rediscovered peaceful sleep.

Later, at 5:45 A.M., the slumbering professor was startled by an earsplitting alarm clock that pushed her out of bed in a daze. She grabbed the silk robe draped on the chair and groggily put one foot after the other toward the bathroom. When there, the wall switch threw a blinding light from the ceiling that tinseled the fixtures and mirror. She squinted and blinked repeatedly until the foggy blur of sleepiness was almost gone. "Gotta' do something about changing to softer bulbs," she drowsily mumbled, while still drowning in sleepiness, pinching her eyes together and shielding them from the penetrating glare. She planned to start her day in an hour.

With the morning temperature rising quickly in San Honesto, Olivia's goal was to get ahead of the daily singe. Dressing hurriedly, she pulled on black leggings and a tank top, and double-knotted her sneakers. Sporting a ponytail and a favorite cap, she hurried to the nearby lakefront for the usual two-mile walk before sunrise.

While walking the lake, Dr. Reece reflected on why she found her home in the L.A. suburb to be the ideal place for her life's work. Just fifteen miles north of Hollywood, San Honesto had a unique vibe. Half the twenty-thousand who lived there held technology jobs specializing in cybersecurity, digital analysis, and forensic investigation or took jobs as security architects and engineers. Still others worked in academia, preparing students for the expected deluge of cyber-driven industries. The decade-long migration of Millenials from east to west typically landed them in places like San Honesto.

As she made her last lap around the lake, Olivia believed no one in the San Honesto (Saint Honest) suburb welcomed the record-shattering heat, where desert-dry lips kissed beer bottles, sipped frozen margaritas, and swallowed tall glasses of lemonade to find relief for parched throats. San Honesto heat also made it hard for students to fight the urge to skip class in exchange for long, lazy days on the Pacific beaches, and where all summer long, young tech-oriented professionals braved incinerate conditions for a quick midday lunch or early dinner.

Today, like so many days at the height of one of the hottest summers on record, the ever-popular college town in suburban L.A. was vibrant: energized with an intense mixture of hormones and testosterone, whipping up every sort of heated dalliance that one could imagine. By all accounts, the valley was in heat.

Chapter 2
Moxie

Later, while driving to the university, Olivia recalled a sobering incident when she was publicly challenged by her first college physics professor. The professor's lack of sensitivity toward her and other students had indelibly shaped her views on teaching. The unconscionable and slanderous act against Olivia was extraordinarily hurtful, and what occurred that disturbing day never left her memory.

"Olivia Reece! Is there an Olivia Reece in here!" The students could hear Professor Hooperman shouting her name as he descended the aisle and scanned the room for signs of her.

"Where is she?" He growled, walking with a noticeable limp. He balanced a large textbook under one arm and carried a tattered leather briefcase overstuffed with protruding books and crumpled papers in his left hand. Every week, he routinely exposed his amusing disorganization to students who overlooked his insensitive conduct to win favor in his class. Predictably, on this day, he was wearing a wrinkled blazer and khaki pants that he apparently owned for years. His teeth, yellowed from smoking, hid behind a bushy, untrimmed mustache that swept upward on the ends, exposing an unpleasant and intimidating scowl.

"Where is Olivia Reece!" He shouted at the audience.

The students were stunned by the loud summons coming from their rumpled instructor. No one dared speak. Hooperman stopped at the podium and noisily dropped his belongings on the long rectangular table used during exams to demonstrate prototypes designed in the campus lab. He shouted once more, "Miss Reece! Miss Reece!" By now he was much louder.

Olivia, dumbfounded at hearing her name blasted across the massive room and doing everything she could to make sense of why he was yelling for her, raised her hand and answered timidly.

"I'm Olivia Reece."

In an instant, the professor spitefully lit into her.

"Miss Reece! There is a university policy that forbids plagiarism. If you don't know what that means, allow me to help you understand. It is lying on a paper or misrepresenting your writing by using the published words of another."

Beginning to anger, but with caution, she asked, "What are you talking about, Dr. Hooperman?"

He yelled in her direction beyond the shocked onlookers, refusing to answer her question.

"And such behavior warrants immediate and permanent dismissal from this university. I will expose you, Young Lady. And this goes for any other student who commits such an act or attempts to do so in this or any other class on this campus!"

As though trying to show that he had been triumphant in his act of reprimand, he stood back with his chest extended, proud to have publicly vilified her.

Olivia was astonished. By this time, some students were whispering reactions to what they witnessed.
Others gasped with surprise, embarrassed for her. It was a bizarre scene. No one stirred.

"This will be a lesson to all of you!" He scornfully looked around the room and waved his finger at dozens of students - their blank expressions staring back at him.

Unsurprisingly, she recoiled. She was pissed. The professor was publicly scolding her. How dare he do such a thing? In her mind, his outrage toward her was absurd and incomprehensible. Prompted by brewing anger, Olivia unleashed fury. Her respect for the older man had instantaneously dissipated in the cloud of words now thrown between them.

"What the hell are you talking about, Dr. Hooperman? What kind of plagiarism are you referring to? I ask respectfully, Sir!" She demanded of him.

Her parents instilled in her the virtue of standing up for what's right, even if it meant losing allies. And although she respected authority, she was not about to be embarrassed in front of her peers, nor be demeaned like a two-year-old, especially when the allegations discriminatingly hurled at her were false.

He shot back vehemently. "You filled your paper on the electromagnetic theory with blatant lies about your connection with Dr. Chin in California! Falsely adding citations of involvement with the recent work at his university was also a big lie. Oh yeah, and the ridiculous lie that he was your mentor. Lies, Miss Reece! Lies!"

"But Dr. Hooperman, why would you say I lied?" She continued, trying to show at least a grain of respect for him. "Why would you assume such a thing without asking me first? It's ludicrous for you to make such an accusation! I cannot believe this! You have to be kidding me!"

The room was hushed as students tuned into the escalating clash between a ranking professor and one of their classmates. The scene had become entertainment for them, and they were not about to miss it.

He hollered. "This is not an assumption! Besides, you don't even know the meaning of ludicrous! Chin would never…"

He coughed, cleared his throat, and came short of the harsh, incendiary words that escaped him without forethought of where he was standing.

"What the hell are you saying!" Olivia's anger had surged to rage. Shocked students waited for the proverbial pin to drop. Silence.

Brian Hooperman stopped shouting the inflamed words and the loathsome criticisms of her were suddenly gone. His puffy hands pressed hard on the worktable to support his weight while his face turned pale. Lashing out at her had taken a turn. No one could've imagined what might happen next.

The young woman's eyes watered. She was livid. But she refused to succumb to any unwarranted drama solicited by someone who appeared out of control. This clash with her teacher was a challenge of her principles and integrity; no hurtful words, not even from him, would dismantle that. Irrespective of his malice she was not going to give him the joy of humiliating her to tears.

"Dr. Hooperman, I am saying this so that everyone in this room is witness to these outrageous comments of yours. First, I don't think I owe you the courtesy of a defense after your ludicrous claims. Yes, Sir, ludicrous!"

Hooperman was mute.

Olivia persisted, "For your information, Dr. Chin is a family friend, whom I met when I was in high school. As you know, he is one of the best in physics!"

Her cutting argument didn't stop there. "For two years, I volunteered with Dr. Chin. Yes, he mentored me! I can prove it, if you wish, by calling him right now! And yes, he's even encouraged me, since I've been here at *your* university. I don't have to lie about working with him and his graduate assistants; it is an honor, you, Dr. Hooperman, never had!"

Hooperman sat down while his face went from white as a sheet to bright crimson. Olivia's scathing comeback was out of character to what he was accustomed when censuring his students in class. In turn, she tore down the professor's ego.

She continued the offensive in reaction to his stinging, taunting words. "I have no reason to lie about something as significant as that. And if you think I've lied, then maybe your contemptible attitude is showing."

Driven by anger, Olivia went further to criticize the baseless indictment. "I am ashamed of you, Dr. Hooperman. I had a helluva lot more respect for you before now!"

After Olivia's heated retort, he stood, rattled and speechless, clinching the table near the scattered books and mountain of papers. The shamed professor desperately surveyed the room, hoping a student would rise in his defense. No one said a word.

"If you'd only check your damn facts before attempting to embarrass any of us, the way your insensitive and arrogant ass does all the time, you wouldn't be standing there with goddamn egg on your face." She fumed. "In my opinion, you've just demonstrated the poorest example of a professor that I've ever seen in my entire life! If you don't trust me to answer you honestly, I strongly advise you to call Dr. Chin. Would you like his number!"

Olivia rushed out of the room and went to the Dean's office. There, she reported Dr. Hooperman's flagrant behavior and the underhanded treatment levied upon her in a classroom of peers. Several students corroborated what happened, describing in detail the reckless actions of the instructor.

A day after she presented her case, the Dean issued a stern reprimand to Hooperman and copied it to Olivia. The letter also stated that Dr. Chin mentored her at the Santa Cruz campus, and he had done so for years.

Not only did the Dean's letter remind Hooperman of the professional behavior required of all university faculty, but he also owed Ms. Reece an apology for the embarrassment he'd unduly caused her.

Brian Hooperman had been humiliated, yet with apparent reluctance, a letter of apology containing only two lines and a hastily scribbled signature came from him. The public scolding by the university administrators also sent a strong message to other faculty. The incident humbled Hooperman, causing him to realize the gravity of his brazen actions and its impact on all students. His callous and intimidating behavior ended. Plus, he had to endure Olivia's presence in his class until the end of the semester. She declined to transfer.

That upsetting day was a harsh lesson for the both of them. Olivia was now more determined to prove her abilities regardless of what others might have assumed about her. Her parents taught her to be strong in her convictions, confident in her resolve, and to confront every crisis head-on without irrational fear. Now, years later in her career, her values remained the same.

As she drove to UST that morning to teach electromagnetic theory, she brushed aside the ugly incident involving Dr. Hooperman and once more buried it in her past.

Dr. Reece reached the campus and snagged the last vacant parking space in the restricted faculty area. From there, it was a quick three-minute walk to her office. She was taken by surprise when she got there. The sudden burst of hot air caught her off guard upon entering the College of Science building, where students were milling around near the entrance. The lobby was stifling, which explained why others weren't inside. Judging from sweat-soaked students and faculty, it was like a sauna on every floor. While cautioned by the potential of unpleasant conditions, Olivia boarded the elevator for the sixth floor. The thermostat in her office blinked ninety-three degrees.

She immediately dialed Ms. Marshall's desk. When Ms. Marshall, the office manager, answered on the first ring, Olivia could barely speak before the middle-aged woman interrupted her.

"Dr. Reece, I know why you've called me. Please don't worry. I've already requested help from maintenance. I'm sorry, but the entire building has an air conditioner problem today, and it feels like this floor is on fire. Maintenance workers are coming up to fix the system soon."

The office manager was contrite. "I know you've come in early for the faculty meeting, Doc. You can rest assured they will fix it long before we start."

"It's okay, Ms. Marshall. I know this is a priority, and the problems you're having with the thermostat are not your fault."

Although grateful for the professor's kind words, the woman continued to express frustration.

"Yes, Dr. Reece, and I'm sorry about it being so hot in your office. My phone hasn't stopped ringing since I arrived at 7:30, with Dr. Bledsoe being the first to call me. There have been tons of complaints. May I get you something cold to drink if that will help?"

"No thanks. Is there any more space downstairs?"

"Dr. Gibson and Dr. Thibodeaux are there,"she answered.

Seeing the perspiration beading on Olivia's bare arms, the office manager continued her recommendations.

"After all, the lab uses that independent temperature control unit. You know, the one used for specialized equipment. But don't forget, you won't have privacy, and you won't have access to your office phone."

"Hey, here's an idea. What if Dean Coleman cancels the faculty meeting? Can she move it to another day since we have this suffocating problem?" Olivia quipped jokingly, easing any tension caused by the rising heat.

"Now. Dr. Reece, you know how Dean Coleman is about this kind of thing; she won't bend when it comes to meetings. I doubt she'd ever think of canceling it."

The office manager's reply was noticeably cheerful. Both women could have easily shared many good words or stiff warnings about their boss. Yet a lot of thoughts were left unspoken on purpose. In spite of her stern management style, nearly everyone in the college had a tremendous fondness for Dean Alexandria Coleman, who was quick to say she didn't take "one damn piece of crap" from anyone. No doubt, she was in charge and overwhelmingly respected, too. For all the right reasons, the Dean was a tough, hard-nosed, no-nonsense administrator who cussed whenever needed but did her best to keep the college's respectable reputation in the right place. She was known for wise leadership, and because of Dean Coleman, the university's College of Science was ranked among the best in the country.

As a smart move, the Dean surrounded herself with top-rated instructors whose resumes were scrutinized and vetted before being offered a professorship at UST. Anyone on the faculty would attest that it was not easy to get hired by Dr. Coleman.

The reputable College received millions for new innovations and scholarships, keeping them on par with many Ivy League universities in the Northeast. Likewise, loyal professors had no interest in leaving for other institutions unless a specialized research or desirable teaching opportunities pushed them elsewhere. Most instructors had been at UST for at least ten years.

"Okay, Ms. Marshall," Olivia said. "I'll check for space in the lab, so if there are any urgent calls, please ring me on my cell phone. By the way, I shot an email reply to Dr. Zane Adams at ECU. So, if he calls, please let me know. I want to speak with him right away."

"Yes, Doc, I will," she agreed and hung up.

It took five minutes to gather everything for her temporary downstairs office. She'd also printed a revised copy of *The Principal Impacts of Linear Momentum and Rotational Motion on Atmospheric Clusters* for the Dean's meeting.

When she reached the office door to go downstairs, Olivia faced a comical challenge. She needed to rethink her exit plan since her purse and laptop made it impossible to grab the doorknob. "I need to get my cellphone off the charger," she grumbled, turning to see it propped on the bookshelf.

Just then, she was off balance. "I need more hands."

When she started to drop everything, Ms. Marshall accidentally pushed the door far too wide when entering the professor's office. The door bumped Olivia.

"Sorry, Dr. Reece. I'm sorry. I didn't mean to hit you. I wanted you to know the Dean's meeting is at eleven-thirty," Ms. Marshall said as she steadied the professor's armload.

"No injuries. I'm okay, Ms. Marshall," she smilingly answered. The professor's clumsy attempt to juggle her belongings and open the heavy door was comical.

"By the way, can you get my phone off the bookshelf and put it in my purse, please? I don't have a way of getting it unless I put this stuff down."

"Sure. No problem," Ms. Marshall responded while reaching for the cord to unleash the phone. She placed it and the charger into a bright red leather case and slid the two devices into Olivia's oversized purse.

"Thanks, Ms. Marshall," she said as she left the office. "You're a lifesaver."

Olivia reached the hallway elevator and did a trick of pushing the down button with her elbow since no one was there to help. Soon, she entered the basement laboratory, which was twenty degrees cooler and filled with others who wanted to escape the stuffy conditions above them.

Finding a remote space to work was difficult, but luck belonged to her. There was a vacant desk in the rear of the room. In an isolated area of the windowless lab, Dr. Kip Thibodeaux, a renowned physicist, and Olivia's closest research ally, was in deep concentration, poring over the pages of a three-inch thick textbook. He looked up when she greeted him.

"Good morning, Partner," he said and smiled, "Welcome to your new office."

Chapter 3
Anticipation

The next day, when Olivia finished a second loop around the lake, Eric was also moving through his routine in the nearby fitness center. The sweat-soaked t-shirt that covered muscular abs and rock-hard biceps meant only one thing - the morning workout was a perfectly sound reason to get up before dawn.

When he finished the last set of reps, he wiped streams of sweat dripping from his forehead and pitched the towel back into the duffel bag. It landed on his cell phone, and again, pleasant and rousing thoughts of meeting Olivia crossed his mind. By now, he couldn't wait to call her.

"Nope, I won't call her until later tonight," he maturely reasoned, innocently tickled by his teenage excitement of seeing her soon. He piled everything into the bag and walked toward the convenient rear exit of the gym.

Although it was minutes after 7:00 A.M., a searing hot day was in the making. Early as it was, the temperature outside the mega fitness complex had already leaped to ninety-four degrees, reminding Californians of the inescapable long hot summer.

"It's going to be blistering out here today," he droned, "and it won't be long before I'll have to turn the lawn sprinklers on at my place."

Yet, feeling hopeful, he gazed upward, searching for the possibility of rain. There were no clouds above except for a few wispy swirls of white slowly drifting westward toward the ocean. Disappointedly, he bemoaned the unbearable summer season. "I've put a lot of money into my place to keep the property value up, and I'm not going to let water restrictions ruin my investment. Oh, hell no!" he swore out loud.

A mindless click of the FOB unlocked his car. Without looking, he tossed his worn duffel onto the back seat. Surprisingly, something made a loud clanging sound. The bag's target was a metal basket full of his newly printed company brochures. They scattered everywhere. His company, *Velocity Engineering*, redesigned its website and the brochures had also been updated. After neatly re-stacking them, he slid onto the leather seat of his car for the short drive home.

Eric steered his two-door out of the parking lot toward the interstate highway and noticed a flashing voicemail reminder on the dashboard. A monotone message said, "Eric, please call your office. We have some questions regarding a recent contract; we need your authorization as soon as possible."

He recalled the upcoming meeting scheduled for late November in Sacramento with *Ergowilst Solutions* Days earlier, he had spoken with Lukas Schmitz, CEO at Ergowilst, to confirm that *Velocity's* proposal was ready for review. Once in the office, the Ergowilst project would be the first thing on his agenda. Nonetheless, he couldn't think of any reasons for concerns. Dismissing more thoughts on the project, he eased into four-lane traffic and accelerated ahead of a long line of approaching cars. He settled in for the ten-minute drive home.

Eric's successful engineering business opened the same day that he celebrated his twenty-eighth birthday. Two low-interest loans and the last of his savings equipped the small office in the San Honesto shopping plaza. He'd also hired a second engineer. So, it's no wonder Ergowilst had become one of Velocity's most lucrative partners, especially since owner Lukas Schmitz sealed sizable projects with Eric's company every year. Fortunately, Eric's consulting and aircraft design firm continued to thrive nearly six years after opening. He was enjoying an increasing annual income thanks to an expansion of loyal clients and partners. Yet, by far, Ergowilst was his most dependable client. He was grateful for his partnership with Lukas, so he was obliged to call him as soon as he reached work.

Finally at home from the gym, he rolled into the garage and dropped the two-car metal door closed. As a single man, he was especially pleased to own a home, which was his private oasis. A year earlier, he bought the property to fit a self-avowed bachelor lifestyle that suited him, and over time, he realized that he'd made a wise purchase. After breaking up with Jasmine, the woman who shared a place with him in Pomona, the thought of getting into another condo was furthest from him. Truthfully, he'd placed a lot of importance on solitude and privacy, and an attached dwelling was not to his liking. His 1800 square-foot house on the outskirts of San Honesto had a spacious main bedroom with a show-stopping bathroom: a custom-built shower, a claw-foot bathtub, and a double sink with high-polished hardware. If there had been time today, a slow, relaxing bath would have been the perfect respite, with hot, steamy water soothing his back and shoulders after a vigorous morning workout. But today, managing his business would not allow him that pleasure.

"Next time," he sighed and reluctantly stepped out of the shower to get a thick terry bath sheet from the walk-in closet. He wrapped the white fabric snugly around his brown torso, soaking up the last few water droplets before they hit the natural stone-tiled floor.

He hurried to get ready for work but was running out of time. Glancing into the mirror, he decided that his shadowy stubble was passable. He skipped shaving.

An incoming call from senior engineer Allen Brinks, interrupted a pace that would've kept him on track to leave in thirty minutes.

"I hope we don't have issues with that last contract."

He pulled his shirt over a splash of cologne and rushed to answer the call. "What's up? He answered promptly.

"Hey, Boss, how ya' doing?"

"Everything is good. What's going on Allen?"

He wanted to get to the purpose of the call. It was not the right time for casual talk with a senior employee. Meanwhile, he was attempting to fix his tie into a half-Windsor knot. He looped it for the second time before getting it right, while also listening to Brinks.

"Just a quick reminder and heads-up for you, Eric. Two reps from Ergowilst Solutions are stopping by today; I'm not exactly sure when they'll arrive. They're supposed to drop some files off for the upcoming Sacramento meeting."

"That's right. I think we're ready for them. Run a quick check to confirm we have enough copies of the proposal. In any case, I don't believe there's reason for us to be concerned, do you?" He earnestly solicited Brinks' input.

The two men were compatible coworkers. What pleased him most were Brinks' efficiency and consistent reliability. He trusted him wholeheartedly as a friend and colleague. The confidence level between the two men was so high that he'd planned to offer Allen a larger share of the company within the coming year.

"Okay, Man." Brinks' response was reassuring.

While listening to the update, Eric belted his cuffed slacks, adjusted the collar on his shirt, and checked his hair in the bathroom mirror as Allen spoke.

"Good. I'll see you in about a half hour, Allen."

Eric had a reputation for being a prodigiously gifted engineer, and his talents became increasingly evident as Velocity expanded its portfolio. His primary business principle remained the same from the first day he started the company: to master his engineering skills and continually expand his client base through hard work. Each year, his bottom line stayed in the black, and he consistently garnered substantial increases in his profit margin. As one of only three aviation engineering firms in San Honesto and the only one in the region with four of the best commercial aircraft designers in the area, his firm generated over eight million annually. His goal was to exceed ten million dollars the following year. The persuasions of success were calling upon Eric to work harder. Minutes after getting dressed, he left for the office.

As one might expect, several women who worked in the shopping plaza and knew of his marital profile shamelessly approached Eric with evocative, risqué offers of home-cooked meals along with unlimited lubricious attention. Their flirting was flattering and equally amusing. More than a dozen times, he found perfume-scented notes on his car's windshield with scribbled phone numbers and salacious offers to meet up somewhere. Coworkers in his close-knit office unmercifully teased him each time a different note awaited his reply.

Unimpressed, every licentiously laced note was tossed aside without thinking of ever responding. It was heartening to know some women viewed him as attractive, but he was not interested in one-night stands with women who didn't have decency or self-respect. He wanted more than that. He hoped for something more meaningful.

On the other hand, it wasn't that he didn't enjoy intimacy just like any other healthy guy; it was just that a string of disingenuous physical encounters didn't appeal to him. Besides, he was a bit old-fashioned regarding the rudiments of fidelity. Perhaps that set him apart from other men in his circles. Even his closest friends considered it odd of him to stick to the outdated tenets of monogamy. But, regardless of his friends' opinions, he did not intend to change his views on romance. Apart from his negative past with Jasmine, he still wanted to experience an authentic, loving relationship with someone else.

When he reached the office and pulled into the reserved parking space, hurtful memories of his failed relationship with Jasmine entered his soul. Bitter thoughts of her brought on a sorrowful blue mood that was difficult to shake. To reckon with unhappiness about his past, Eric typically stayed in the office for unusually long hours, as it would be today - many times, remaining there twelve to fourteen grueling hours a day. In some ways, time at work was a way to mask his loneliness and empty heart. Today, however, his thoughts kept returning to Olivia until it was time to go home.

By early evening, interstate motorists surrendered to clogged, multi-lane traffic that slowly crawled in both directions. When he left work and merged onto the busy highway toward home, his displeasure for California freeways was apparent, and for a short moment, he missed a slower life in the South.

As his car trudged along the roadway, he thought of the afternoon meeting with Ergowilst Solutions. Thankfully, with Allen's careful planning, he was prepared to review the project details. Ergowilst engineers spoke highly of Velocity's expertise and promised additional contracts. It was good news for everyone on his team, especially for Eric. When finally at home off the busy freeway, he hurried inside to unwind.

After a quick shower and catching up on local news, he fell asleep on the couch but woke up a short time later to a sitcom that he considered a failed comedy. It always started with a silly, off-color punchline that was senseless. He shook his head at the silliness on the flat screen and, without prompting, knew it was time for bed. But, before turning in, he had one more thing to do. "Yes, I want to do this. It's now or never."

He autodialed and waited. The phone rang four times.

He was about to hang up when she, at last, answered. Olivia curiously greeted the caller since she had not saved his number.

"Hello, this is Dr. Reece. How can I help you?"

"Hi, its Eric. Eric Blake."

She was glad to get the call but wanted to keep ole school dating rules in mind by not sounding too excited.

"How was your day?"

"It was a good day, thanks." She casually answered.

He didn't want to miss the chance to see her again and wasted no time asking. "That's great to hear. Now, ah…dinner tomorrow night, maybe?" He was wishful. He said, "That is if you're available."

"Yes, I am available. And yes, I would love to go," Olivia answered.

Chapter 4
Contemplation

By the next afternoon, the university was a ghost town. Parking lots were almost bare, with a few cars abandoned by students who carpooled to nearby bars to start their weekend celebration ritual. Olivia's students rushed from the lecture hall to join the campus crowd in the age-old practice that was repeated in college towns everywhere. When the room cleared, her graduate assistant hurriedly handed off a USB flash drive of lecture notes and student feedback.

"Have a good weekend, Dr. Reece," she said while closing the door. By then, Olivia couldn't gather her things fast enough. She had already switched from a lecture on electromagnetic waves to anticipating a date with someone new.

On leaving campus, thoughts of David Ames, her ex-boyfriend, intruded upon her. It had been a while since the breakup, but she needed David to vanish from her memory for good. The disastrous romantic experience had jaded her, and the affair was an unpleasant occurrence that wounded her emotionally. Over time, the thing she had with David proved to be an inexpressible failure. Long, unfiltered conversations with her friend, Lora, had helped her gain the courage to walk away from the ill-fated relationship.

The unstable ride with David also helped to amplify her passion for teaching. A committed relationship was unthinkable at the time. Besides, his callous and hurtful scars remained long after her time with David ended.

She couldn't figure out why the hell she stayed with him so damn long.

As she drove home, the anticipation of going out with Eric felt promising, trusting it to be nothing like her last romantic debacle. No other man could possibly be as disappointing as the one from her recent past, at least she hoped.

Along the way home from UST in rush-hour traffic, a fire truck with its shrilling siren, pushed through bunched cars on the crowded highway. Drivers stopped and edged closer to the guardrails, allowing the red truck with flashing lights to force its way through. During the traffic pause, Olivia's cell phone rang. She answered, knowing who it was.

"Hello, Mom," she said as Lillie's ID scrolled on the dashboard. "I'll have to shout because emergency vehicles are going by. There has to be a serious fire somewhere. What's going on with you?"

Lillie went straight to inquisition mode without responding to Olivia's lengthy greeting. "How are you, Sugar? I haven't heard from you in two days. Is everything okay?"

"Oh yeah, Mom. It's going great," Olivia answered Lillie. Her mother could inflate anything if she tried hard enough.

"Really, Honey?" Lillie curiously questioned her daughter. She was wondering about the hint of excitement in her daughter's voice.

"Oh, nothing special. I had a good day with my students. This weekend is looking good, too."

"That's nice, Baby."

"Yeesss, Momma."

She rarely called her mother Momma since Lillie disliked the moniker Her self-proclamation was mom and not momma.

"What is it you plan to do, Olivia Beatrice Reece?" Lillie's witty retort was a comeback for calling her Momma. Between them, at all times, the repartee was playful.

"Maybe I'll do some work at my place or catch a movie with Lora or go on a date with a new friend, who knows what'll happen." She answered her mother, dividing concentration among Lillie, thoughts of Eric, and being stuck in the endless chain of cars.

"What about you, Mom?" She asked, wanting her mother to find something else to talk about.

"Not sure," Lillie answered, eager to unload the day's events. "Your father wants to go to the antique mall tomorrow, and I'm not ready to look for more junk to clutter this house. Although nineteenth-century furniture is what I'd love to find there."

Lillie's daughter rolled her eyes. She couldn't comprehend her parent's fascination with old stuff - of what seemed like dated junk, odds, and ends they found in crowded, funky antique stores rarely shopped by anyone outside their age bracket. She presumed it had something to do with being from an older generation and holding on to memories of a familiar past. Lillie and Edward spent much of their antique shopping time casually exploring cluttered haunts along the coast. During the time of socializing with shop owners and browsing stores, they bought unusual, and more often, useless things they neither wanted nor needed. If the occasional finds didn't work out, they ended up being donations to local thrift shops.

"I'm convinced you and Dad always enjoy the adventures, don't you?"

"If you say so," Lillie responded to Olivia's comment. Her mother was trying hard to show constraint. She inhaled, then released a shallow breath, allowing an exhale to filter through her daughter's car speakers. Admittedly, she enjoyed weekend outings with her husband, but many good times were lost in the stumbling blocks that their marriage had encountered in years past.

She finished the call with her daughter.

"I need to call your Aunt Doris. She's going with us tomorrow. Take care, Honey."

"Okay, Mom. Love you," said Olivia. At that moment, she felt a profound love for her mother. The feeling sweetly and unexpectedly appeared from nowhere and remained long after she'd said goodbye to Lillie.

"Bye, Darling. Love you, too." Lillie responded.

The young professor sighed casually and stretched an arm beyond the steering wheel as she drove along. Her voice command turned on the satellite radio, which infiltrated the car with a funky hip-hop tune she had danced to back in college. Mouthing the lyrics and bobbing her head to the beat, she noticed passengers in the next lane watching and smiling. Olivia responded with a wave.

She arrived home, entering through the garage. Two hours was the time she had to get ready for a date with Eric.

"What am I gonna' wear? Red dress? Black dress?" She was torn between the two colors. If she had only known more about Eric, deciding what to wear would've been a helluva' lot easier.

"I have one time to knock this date out of the park," she vowed while sorting through jewelry pieces. One chunky necklace matched the red dress, but a single pearl on a sterling chain added the right classic touch to the black A-line dress. "No matter what, I'm giving it a good shot and this dress and pearls will help."

Meanwhile, not far from Olivia's place, Eric arrived home and turned the music on. Months earlier, he'd installed an audio system with speakers permeating smooth sounds in every room. One of his favorite soulful R&B tracks was spinning and getting him fired up for his night out. He animatedly crooned the lyrics, and his face contorted with every high-pitched note while thinking about going out after a long hiatus from dating.

Two years had passed after his departure from a woman he'd joyfully dismissed from his life. Since the relationship with Jasmine had impacted him so negatively, he'd promised never to get seriously involved with anyone else again. Even so, he was enticed by Olivia. She was like no other woman he'd ever met, and he couldn't figure out exactly why she was pulling him in her direction.

"It's funny, though," he reasoned, "you never know what will happen as you travel through life. Surprises are at every turn along the journey." He was feeling good about what the evening might bring.

Petaluma Avenue was five miles from Eric's house, so he switched on the navigation system to get there quickly. He remembered their first conversation about being on time, so he was willing to do almost anything to be at her doorstep as promised; not one minute later.

On Petaluma, nervousness arose in him. He wanted their first night out together to be the beginning of many dates afterward. Earlier in the day, he made reservations at The Moon Eclipse, one of the finest restaurants in Long Beach. The popular eatery was on the exclusive south end of Locust Avenue, and the drive would take under an hour to get there. Although he wasn't familiar with the restaurant, his coworker, Brinks, had given it a top rating.

His plan was to drive west, then southward along the shore during sunset. He also hoped for light Friday night traffic that would bring about easy conversation.

Eric glanced at his dashboard navigation map to re-check the arrival time at her condominium and realized that he was three minutes away. When he got there, a massive wrought iron gate guarded the entrance.

Two cars entered the gated complex ahead of him. He eased forward and was met by an affable guy about thirty-five years old who greeted him with a smile. When the guard tipped his cap and pressed a button inside the small checkpoint building, the large metal gate spread wide for Eric to roll through.

The secluded neighborhood had immaculately manicured lawns with rows of trimmed shrubs bordering sidewalks and driveways. Black wrought-iron lampposts illuminated the well-kept grounds in the exclusive community known as a popular haven for white-collar professionals.

A half-block from the entrance, four numbers, twenty-two zero five, were spotted on a mailbox near the sidewalk. Once out of the car, he hurried up a half-dozen steps to a front door with a brass, lion's head doorknocker and a thick welcome mat pushed against the threshold where he timorously stood.

He nervously rang the bell and waited for her to answer. Inside, Olivia's high heels clicked across the polished wood floor toward the door. The doorknob turned. He sucked air and waited. When the door opened, Eric was awestruck. She was even more beautiful than before. The red sleeveless knit dress that she ended up choosing drew attention to her toned arms and shapely legs. The bright colored dress enhanced the beauty of her brown skin.

"Hey," she said behind an inviting smile. "Come on in. I'm going to take my doberman out to the patio. I will be right back."

He had not heard a dog barking but reacted to the surprising announcement within a split second. Wearing a baffled expression, he asked, "Whoa! Do you have a doberman?" His wary eyes cautiously searched the well-kempt room.

Olivia was amused by Eric's reaction. "I'm sorry. I'm just kidding you."

As they crossed the room, she delicately touched his arm and reassured him.

"I was only teasing you, Eric. I don't have a ferocious pet. I don't even own a fishbowl." She said, "My dad told me to play out the doberman ruse as an advantage over anyone who might be here without an invitation." She walked toward the kitchen to offer him something to drink.

He mockingly asked, "Is it safe? This drink, I mean?" He teased with a smile, now more at ease.

"Of course, it is. What can I get for you?" asked Olivia, wanting to stop his hesitation.

"Whatever you have is okay with me." He answered and followed her into the kitchen, all the while taking in a whiff of intoxicating perfume that wafted around her as she moved.

"You have a nice place," he remarked, looking around the spacious condo and sipping from a glass of white wine.

"Is there a balcony upstairs?" He took another sip of the chilled chardonnay and gestured upward.

"Yeah, it's overlooking the courtyard. Is the wine okay for you?"

"Yes. Thanks."

He swallowed more wine while trying to stave off first-date jitters. His lips stayed on the rim of the glass as he watched her move about the room. She was graceful. Her lithe moves reminded him of weightless thistledown in an open field. The whole scene was enticing for him, and he couldn't put off staring at her. Her beauty struck him, and he found himself adoring everything about her.

He took two more sips of wine to escape fixation on her and casually checked out her home. A wire basket was filled with golden apples, red plums, and bananas on the kitchen counter. Modern art graced walls covered in warm vanilla paint. Sculptures, oil paintings, and unusual artistic exposés revealed her interest in progressive, offbeat 21st-century artists. The décor embodied a modern-day eclectic style. Anyone could see that none of the furniture pieces matched, yet the bold merger of textures and patterns mixed with rich earth colors created a sleek, sophisticated urban ambiance. But he couldn't keep his eyes off her. Her pleasing appearance intrigued him.

"What kind of music do you like, Olivia?" he questioned, carefully folding the napkin and placing the long-stemmed goblet on a brown and beige coaster, then waiting for her to answer. He noticed how easy it was to say her name.

"I love music." A smile curled her thick, red lips when she answered him. "It doesn't matter, rhythm and blues, contemporary or traditional jazz, hip-hop, classical, and even some country and western, but not much of that," she confessed. "My girlfriend, Lora McGowan, taught me everything I should know about the C&W genre. Most of those songs are about love and heartbreaks - you know, just like R&B."

"Yes."

"Yeah. Country music is what you might want to check out sometime." Olivia laughed subtly.

He rested an elbow on the counter and cupped his chin to look closely at her before she looked away. He'd found himself staring at a lovely woman with the sexiest eyes he'd ever seen. Bashful but suddenly having no restraint, he blurted out, "You have gorgeous eyes."

And she, lowering her face in reaction to his flattering words, responded in a voice that was near to inaudible.

"Thank you."

Being near him was instantly intoxicating and the unexpected blush momentarily jailed her senses. For a seemingly long time, they held onto a gravid pause that channeled heated sensuality between them. Olivia's charm was powerful. For him, the moment was an odd, inexplicable feeling because he was caught between excitement to learn more about her while also being cautiously reserved about moving too fast. Yet, somehow, he knew he was where he wanted to be in that entrancing instance. Now, though, he needed to return to reality, so he awkwardly announced, "I think we should hit the road. The drive to The Moon Eclipse will take about an hour. By the way, I hope the restaurant choice is alright with you."

"Oh, sure," she answered.

"How about this? Why don't we take the coastal drive there and back? It'll be a scenic ride, and there will be less traffic."

"It's a great plan. Let's do it." Olivia said while grabbing her purse.

"What's your favorite music," she asked him, easing onto the passenger seat. She wanted to know more about what made Eric Blake so appealing. He, too, was interested in their developing conversation and wanted more. He closed the passenger door for her and walked around the car to get in. After latching his seatbelt and being thoughtful about what should be said next, he answered her.

"Well, I'm a Southerner, and old-school music is what I enjoy. You know, like R&B love songs." He went on to say, "Sorry, Ma'am, can't say I find those classical tunes by them guys like Bach and Vivaldi excitin'. I guess I'm not refined like other folks when it comes to music. Let me apologize to you, Ma'am."

He was making fun of himself, mocking with a slow Southern accent. And to get a smile from him, his date offhandedly chimed in with a Pacific coast southern 'California' drawl of her own, "Yes, Sirrrr."

Pretty soon, Olivia's inhibitions were melting away, and any precautions she sensed when meeting him were gone. She was starting to like the good-natured man sitting next to her.

"He's a likable guy so far," she thought, gazing off into the distance toward the sunset.

The night was ideal for the hour-long drive to the restaurant. The arrival of dusk unwrapped an endless spray of stars dotting a cast-ironed sky that swallowed a golden sinking sun. God had created an idyllic evening for them.

"Tell me about your business as an aircraft designer and why here in San Honesto?"

"So, our company does aircraft architectural design, something like floor plans for a house. For instance, we specialize in cockpits and passenger seating plans. We leave the mechanical details to our partners. I've been on the West Coast for years and decided to open my firm here in San Honesto."

"I didn't know you were in the plaza."

"No problem. We don't make a big display of what we do."

"My goal is to get my own building in about a year."

Olivia smiled, "I see. That's probably a good business decision."

It was evident that he'd begun to genuinely like her and was thinking of the next thing to say. He wanted to continue the conversation.

"It looks like UST is getting more students. What's going on over there?"

"Yes, that's right, Eric. Enrollment is up. A lot of students come here because of our science programs. In the last decade, some of the sharpest minds in science, mathematics, and cyber technology worldwide have been enrolling with us."

"Where do they come from?"

"From everywhere: North and South America, Africa, Asia, and Europe. Our campus is globally diverse. Quite a number of the students who would've gone to Ivy League Northeast schools are coming to us now."

"What's the reason behind that?"

"I think it is because we have one of the best research reputations in the country. Most of our cyber technology and robotics grads end up with damn good salaries in many of the technology-driven regions all over the world. And here in California, we are so close to Silicon Valley, which gets our students ready for those specialized industries."

"I want to know more about the professor, aka Dr. Reece."

"Humm, what is there to say? Nothing special. I teach Physics."

He laughed easily. "A Physics prof, huh?"

"Yes. I focus on particle physics and how it interfaces with cyber security. Do you know much about that?"

"Definitely not as much as you, and I'd better not try explaining it. Fill me in."

"Here is a simple explanation without making it confusing," she grinned and went on. "Particle physics looks at the nature of particles that make up matter; how can I say this, particles with mass and radiation, which are massless particles, or what we call radiation."

"Sounds complicated, but my background as an engineer actually gives me some idea of what you do," he hesitantly reacted to her explanation.

"Look at it this way. When we think of particles related to scientific study, we're considering distinctive types of teeny, tiny objects like protons, or let's see, like the dust on your dashboard here."

"Sorry, I actually meant to clean the dash," he grinned embarrassingly. "But I'm trying to follow you."

"You see when studying particle physics, we tend to go even further by looking at the smallest detectable particles that cannot be reduced anymore. Therefore, by examining the fundamental force fields that cannot be further reduced to explain those particles."

She continued. "The bulk of my interest is in the excitations of the quantum fields that essentially govern their interactions. This, in turn, gives us greater understanding of quantum mechanics that directly impact cybersecurity."

"Man, that's pretty heavy and way over my head." He joked, "You'd probably give me an F if I were your student."

"Nonsense. You'd likely be among the best if you were in my class."

Though smiling, he didn't look at her while reacting

to the compliment and steering his car into the right lane ahead of traffic. The exit to South Locust Avenue was up next.

Getting to the restaurant in fifty-five minutes with help from the GPS navigation won praise from Eric. Olivia was warmly humored by his apparent interest in the computerized aspects of his car and the eccentric fascination he had with technology. Watching him caused her to think that he was a little geeky and probably quite intelligent, yet not self-absorbed or full of himself. She liked that.

An adolescent-looking female, perhaps no more than eighteen years old, eagerly approached the car as it stopped at the valet parking entrance lined with Ferraris, Bentleys, BMWs, and Mercedes Benzes. Her long blonde hair with pink highlights messaged her youthfulness.

The couple smiled slyly at one another, trying to figure out the adequacy of the young restaurant greeter. He winked at his beautiful companion and whispered. "I hope she knows how to drive."

"Me, too," Olivia responded, returning his wink.

He stretched his eyes upward, casting lines of concern to appear on his forehead. For a fleeting moment, the behavior made him look serious. He noted the valet's name tag, seemingly cautious about someone else handling his vehicle.

The young blonde helped Olivia get out of the car. By then, Eric was standing next to the driver's door, waiting to hand over his keys.

"Welcome to the Moon Eclipse." The woman pointed them toward the arched breezeway. "As soon as you're inside, the maître d' will take good care of you. I hope you enjoy your evening."

"Thanks," Eric said, palming the valet with a twenty. They both could see that the young woman was overjoyed by Eric's generosity.

"Thanks so much, Sir. Thanks!" She persisted. "If there is anything else I can do to assist you tonight, please don't hesitate to let me know. My name is Sandy."

"That's fine, Sandy. Thank you," Eric said and gently circled his arm around Olivia's waist.

Their first stop inside the popular restaurant was the Moon Bar and Lounge. They'd arrived thirty minutes before the reservation and needed to wait for their table.

The sound of chattering patrons floated from the dimly lit bar, while on a small stage, a spotlight fell upon a voluptuous woman crooning smooth jazz lyrics and running her fingers across the keys of a black lacquered Baby Grand. An emerald dress dipped sensuously low with a sequined neckline, hinting at the ampleness of the singer's breasts. Although the sexy dress caused male patrons to cast lustful eyes upon her, the intense songs of love were what listeners had come to enjoy. Eric took Olivia's hand, leading as they followed the maître d' into the lounge.

The man with thinning, silver hair led them to a minibar, where Napa Valley Merlot poured out of frosted chilled bottles. From the bar, they could see the ever-popular and often-toured Rainbow Harbor. In the distance offshore, hundreds of stark-white yachts, some with lights flickering on upper decks, bobbed on tight anchors along the dock. The Harbor, her date casually explained, had a reputation of one of the most visited places in California. He knew a lot about the history of Long Beach, in part, he said, because of working odd jobs during his college days. For a short while, as he shared humorous secrets of his youthful past, they sipped more wine until the table was ready.

When seated for dinner, Olivia's eyes wandered in the cozy upscale setting. It was, in two words, tastefully elegant. The ceiling appeared to be more than ten feet above them. Tables, spaced for privacy, glowed from the shimmer of white candlelight placed near red-clay carafes of chilled wine. Without exchanging glances with each other, they scanned the lengthy wine list and the ten-page, leather-bound menu highlighting the night's special entrée'.

"What's looking good to you, Olivia?"

"I'm not sure yet. Don't know," She answered him while flipping the pages and finding it hard to concentrate, knowing his eyes were on her.

Throughout dinner, the conversation was easy. As it turned out, Christmas and Thanksgiving were special times for his family. His posture softened as he talked about being an only child and how his mother taught him to swim when he was five. He loved the water and fishing was one of his favorite pastimes.

"So, tell me one of your big fish stories. People who fish have at least one." She stretched her arms wide apart in a grand gesture, pleased with the way talking of his family relaxed him.

He sheepishly commented, "I've caught eight or nine exceptionally good-sized fish before. Five lakes are within fifteen or twenty minutes of my folk's house, including one of em' a short distance behind our property."

"Really?" Her eyes latched onto him as more wine flowed. He seemed happy to share one remembrance, then another.

"My dad and I would fish for hours, sometimes cooking them straight out of the water. Washing them first, of course." He expected a squeamish reaction to his cooking confession. Yet, to his surprise, she appeared genuinely moved by his stories, hanging on to every word and asking more questions as they ate.

Two hours later, they left the restaurant holding hands. The valet brought the car around just as they reached the curb.

Traffic in Long Beach had dwindled as he steered past cars merging toward the interstate onramp. He maneuvered to the outer lane, making sure he didn't miss the exit that would take them to the coastline. He intended to take the longest route back to San Honesto because he was not ready to say goodnight.

During the drive home, they discovered more about each other and how much they had in common. There was plenty talk of career aspirations, religious beliefs, and political interests. Warm compatibility was developing.

Before long, they pulled into her driveway. At the front door, the couple fell awkwardly silent, unsure whether to end the evening with the first kiss. Instead, she hugged him gently, pressed her lips to his cheek, and whispered, "This has been nice, Eric. Thank you so much for a fun evening."

Swayed by her touch and the gentleness in her voice, he responded, "I'm hoping we will do this again. I had a good time, too. What if I give you a call soon?"

Her luminous brown eyes returned his hopeful gaze and uttered, "Yes, Eric, I'd like that."

After making sure she was locked in safely, he returned to his car, satisfied with the evening. "I hope we can do this again," he remarked to himself as he started the car and drove away. He could smell her lingering fragrance as he approached the on-ramp toward home.

"Yes. I want to see her again."

Chapter 5
Simpatico

Olivia's close friend, Lora McGowan, was not happy. She wasn't convinced the plumbing company had given her a fair price to clean her flooded basement. Her personality often proved, as in this case, that she could be candid about anything she disagreed with, like the pricey estimate from the man cleaning her floor.

"Two thousand dollars! Why so damned much! I cannot believe this job is costing me that freaking much!" Lora reacted to what she was told.

The plumber started to explain but stopped mid-sentence when she raised her hand to cut him off. All along, he was calm and didn't budge on the charges. Still, she was not about to give in, and for a few long seconds, Lora's cold, unflinching stare-down with him resembled a wild west standoff.

"Considering the time you have wasted here today, it seems YOU should be paying me! It's Saturday, for Pete's sake," she shrieked. "You started this job early this morning. Look at the time. It's close to 4:30 in the afternoon! This is unreasonable!"

She continued to spike one criticism after another at the stoic serviceman who held constraint but also showed her the itemized bill on his iPad along with a paper invoice for her records. Lora eyeballed her suspicions toward the plumber; in defense, her gestures bounced off of him as if he had experienced customer scrutiny before. Refusing to concede to the charges, Lora pitched the controversial invoice onto a damaged table, which had to be thrown out with many other things.

The plumber was annoyed with the battery of questions from Lora, especially since she'd signed consent for him to do the job. In that frustrating instance, he wished for other jobs that he declined for this one.

During the polemic, unmerciful onslaught from Lora, his assistant gathered a pile of soaked rugs, dumped them into a large black plastic garbage bag, and stacked it next to four others overflowing with wet books, soggy clothing, and old pillows. Everything had to be discarded, including many possessions having sentimental meanings from her childhood home in Kentucky.

Meanwhile, Lora followed him and his noisy machine around the room, avoiding the bright orange extension cord that wound around the basement floor, "I tell you what, why don't you let me find someone else to finish this job, and we can straighten the differences out later. I know my insurance will cover this, but I need immediate satisfaction right now, and you're not giving it to me! This charge is too much!"

Her angered breathing shot toward the indifferent man fidgeting with the broken pipes. He ripped several pieces of rusted and mangled metal tubing from the wall without looking her way. The damaged scraps of metal hit the floor noisily. By now, his brewing irritation with her was on the brink of spilling, just like the water that covered her basement floor. Lora knew finding someone else with his qualifications was useless at that hour of the day. Unmistakably, though. she was at odds with him. She left the basement.

Upstairs, she grabbed the phone from the kitchen counter and called Olivia. who answered on the second ring. "Hey, Girlfriend. What's going on with you?" Lora asked, frustrated with the tortoise pace of the workers below.

"Nothing much. I've just opened my files. I plan to spend some of the afternoon analyzing and adjusting my data. London is coming up soon."

"Oh yeah, for sure." Lora answered, "I'm the first to agree with you, my Bestie."

Olivia idly scrolled through eight pages on the computer screen as she listened, looking for errors before continuing the analysis. As she came close to finishing her detailed work, some of the data points needed more clarification. She had successfully derived data from years of effort, and the authenticity and integrity of her research mattered. Olivia also expected her contributions to the upcoming NASA substation project to validate her specialized work on quantum cryptography and its influence on cybersecurity. Importantly, she was getting closer to developing a distinct encryption key, with the help of William Gibson, to make the NASA substation satellite secure.

Like a pro, an empty ink cartridge was lobed into the wicker trash basket across the room, and, at the same time, she listened as Lora agonized over her grim situation.

"Guess what kind of data I'll have to analyze," Lora groaned.

"What's that?" Olivia asked, while twirling a ballpoint pen between her fingers.

"A damaged pipe in my basement exploded and

caused a serious mess over the entire floor. It doesn't look good, and beyond that, the repairman says I'm looking at about two grand or more to clean it up." Her comments implied suspicions of the repairman's surprising figures.

"Won't your insurance take care of it for you?" Olivia asked, hoping for a better impression of Lora's predicament.

"I'm sure it will, but I hate paying more than I need to."

Lora's mood was not good. She was trying to figure out what should be done to resolve the downstairs problem. For a moment she had regrets about having a basement since they were rarely found anywhere in the entire state. But to her it was the perfect asset for storage.

"I guess everything will be fine. What about you? How was your hot date? You didn't call to fill me in."

"Oh. I forgot. My bad."

"That tells me it was so awesome you're keeping the details from me, or it was so awful that you are too damned embarrassed or disappointed to weep on my shoulder. Which one is it?"

Olivia spoke slowly to stir up her friend's curiosity. She was being playfully roguish. "Well, Lora, he was soooooooo incredible. The night was the best I've had with anyone in a long, long time. To be honest, he was kinda' interesting. Can you believe that in this age of dating?"

"What do you mean by that?"

"He was a first-rate gentleman. He was pleasant, and talking with him was very easy. And, get this, he wasn't self-absorbed or boring. We went to a very nice restaurant in Long Beach. It's a high-end place. It was huge." She raised her hands as if Lora could see her gestures through the phone.

"What's its name?" Lora interrupted.

"It? It what?" Olivia asked. She was lost in the good memories of her recent date.

"No. I was not getting personal, Girlfriend." She had to laugh at her unintended faux pas. "The name of the restaurant, Woman!"

"Oh. It's called The Moon Eclipse. Have you heard of it?"

"Yes. It's on Locust. I know of it. I've never been there, but they say it's a ritzy spot. How was it?"

"Yes. It was definitely a five-star restaurant. It had the perfect atmosphere and everything was just right," Olivia confirmed.

The close friends went through the usual girlfriend sharing moments, with Olivia filling Lora in on spicy details and omitting memorable moments she wanted to keep to herself.

She told Lora that after the first date, she had become fond of him, and he was showing signs of being different from her disagreeable ex, David.

Lora reacted to Olivia's excitement by saying, "You've needed to hit the reset button in your love life for a while. Could be the right time to do it."

"You are entirely correct. But I'm not planning to get serious with anyone until my work is complete and my findings get published in a ranking international journal, and the NASA substation is finally launched. After that, I will go to the Caribbean to sip rum and submerge in a glistening tropical sunset."

The two women giggled at the notion of Olivia's saucy island adventure. They loved the excitement that went with traveling together.

"Count me in," said Lora.

Dr. Lora McGowan, blessed with a voluminous mane of kinky, reddish-brown hair and sparkling jade eyes gifted from her mother's genes, was one of the most revered agronomists in the state; ergo, her list of credentials as a scientist was an unusual conversation starter whenever introduced to new acquaintances. It was hard to resist Lora's magnetic personality. Anyone who met her for the first time was impressed that she was a praised scientist in an obscure yet indispensable field. Likewise, Lora enjoyed answering questions about dirt and its impact on the food chain. Her confidence in science was undisputed and audaciously bold.

Typically outspoken and always honest, she quickly dismantled primitive, antediluvian ideas of gender-locked careers. And with all of this, she was a lovely woman. No one could imagine a woman with such beauty researching corn or potatoes.

Olivia valued her friend, Lora, who, until a year ago, had her share of off and on romances. Despite her dazzling good looks and intellect, Lora once offhandedly claimed her romantic drawbacks were caused by not having a father in her life when growing up in a rural town, but she quickly deemed the theory baseless rhetoric. Her childhood had actually been blessed with more than enough endearing male role models. Lora's African American father, a career soldier, was killed in combat before she turned seven. He'd perished during a bombing attack on a convoy in Afghanistan, and his death devastated her entire family. Consequently, Lora's mother, who had defied cultural norms and married outside of her ethnicity, decided not to remarry, returning home to live with her parents in Eastern Kentucky.

Lora, who garnered wide respect in the field of agriculture, instantly spoke her mind when a man didn't meet her standards. Guys who came on to her in the wrong way were ditched before they ever got through the gate of a tightly guarded heart. Despite a few relationship turnovers, Lora eventually met Keith Collins, a kind-hearted man whom she had dated now for nearly a year. As an Army veteran with ten years of service, he was charmingly attracted to the potency of Lora's grit and outspoken personality.

Unmistakable, though, was the affinity between Olivia and Lora. Anyone could tell there was shared debt and real friendship. They met by chance at a science conference and immediately hit it off after having to pair in one of the silly icebreaker activities. Two years later, their friendship bond was a blessing; unconditional trust was mutual, as it was revealed in their talks, like this one.

"Well, I hope everything works out today for you and your basement issue, Lora," said Olivia finally.

"And I hope it works out for you and Eric. He sounds like a nice man," she responded. "By the way, Bessie, Adisa, and I are getting together next Wednesday night for drinks and pasta. Are you interested in meeting up with us?"

"Yeah, just let me know where to meet you. That sounds good. Let's talk tomorrow."

Right after Olivia returned the phone to the charger, it rang again. Glancing over her shoulder, she could see Lillie was calling.

"What is Mom up to now?"

She answered the call before the last ring, turning to shut the computer down for a while.

"Hey, Mom. How's it going?"

Positioning the phone under her chin, Olivia walked to the balcony, where the afternoon sun warmed her.

"Pretty good today, Dear. Nothing much is happening here. I've asked your aunt Doris to go shopping with us after lunch."

"How'd you manage that?" Olivia kept talking as she lowered herself onto the wicker chaise tucked in the corner of her upperstairs porch. The summer breeze cooled her skin as the wind flutter disturbed a cluster of plants in clay pots in the spacious room. Dark brown Italian tile matched sailcloth, thickly-cushioned furniture. The balcony had an exotic tropical air. After two years in the condo, it had become her haven for relaxation and mindful reflection.

"I'm sure I've made a mistake since Doris has decided we're going to some different places to find bargains," her mother colorfully exclaimed. "What have I done, Olivia?"

Lillie's daughter got up and moved to a spot nearest the balcony door, adjusted the blinds to block rays of sunlight hitting her face, and sat down once again. She raised her legs and plopped them on the matching hassock pushed against the rattan chair.

The women laughed together, conceding that Doris was a one-of-a-kind dealmaker whose proclivity for searching to get discounts on just about everything was definitely unmatched. Everyone in the family loved Doris, but she could be a piece of work, as Olivia's dad affectionately described his only sister.

"How are things going for you, Olivia?"

"Lora and I had a long chat this morning. She has basement complications today. But everything is fine with me. Why do you ask?" Olivia considered the nature of her mother's motives for questioning her.

When answering, Lillie glanced up and noticed a small crack in the kitchen ceiling as she thought of Lora's troublesome homeowner's situation. A mental note was made to have Edward take care of it.

In answer to Olivia's question, Lillie said, "Making sure you're alright. No problem with a mother hen looking after her baby chick, is there?"

She didn't want to sound nosy, but concern for Olivia's emotional well-being was important. From her own experiences, Lillie was fully aware of the sting of love and how overwhelmingly painful it was to those who experienced the cutting effects of it.

"Hey, Mom, I'm thirty-three years old. I'd say that I'm a very mature chick, wouldn't you agree?"

Lillie didn't respond. Olivia went on. "But if you're trying to get a report on my recent date, I actually had a nice time."

Within that moment, nothing was said… and the air between them was filled with a perceptible hush.

"Humm, I see." Her mother's eventual reaction was constrained. "That is wonderful, Sweetie. You'll tell me more sometime, won't you? I do hope he is nicer than that dreadful David Ames you dated for so long."

One could hear the despising sentiment coming from Lillie. Undoubtedly, she didn't care for David, and she was often shamelessly honest and condescendingly outspoken to her daughter about him.

"Mom, David, and I just didn't make it, but...he was not exactly dreadful either. Saying that he was dreadful may be a stretch." Pausing for a second, she continued.

"Mom, where do you find such words like dreadful anyway, maybe from soap operas? David just saw the world differently. I thought he was inflexible. He thought I was too ambitious and we needed to move on from each other."

Without question, David, her Ex, had been much too obstinate, and in Olivia's mind, Machiavellian, to be exact. He had become increasingly controlling and manipulative and was unrelenting in his contempt for Olivia's passionate investment in her career. He frequently opined disapproval of her appetite for research and related travel. In the scheme of things, what she wanted did not fit his idea of the traditional couple and to satisfy him she would have to change her attitude about their relationship. In reality, their acutely superficial bond was all about him, and not them.

At first, she thought of his 'pretended devotion' to her as heartwarming, but in the end, Olivia caught on to the detrimental impact he was having on her license of independence. Initially, she had been needy of his approval and attentiveness. After twenty-three months, however, the dubious tie to David was severed when she finally realized how much her self-worth mattered.

Moreover, it mattered more than their occasional, disingenuous intimacy. She was relieved when they decided to break up, and a huge burden was lifted.

Lillie's subtle agreement interrupted her daughter's derisive reflections on David. "You're right, Olivia."

"Right." Olivia felt the need to go on, so she did.

"David and I were different. Extremely different. It's just that I realized that a whole lot later than I should have. He constantly questioned my ambitions and would turn bellicose when I tried to defend my dreams. It was a real problem."

"Bellicose. Humm... isn't that close to my soap opera word dreadful?" Lillie laughed, "Sweetheart, he seemed self-indulgent whenever we saw him. And secretive, too. Your father was always suspicious of his motives. Now, who is this new person? What's his name? Tell me, what is he like?"

"His name is Eric Blake if you must know. He owns Velocity Engineering here in San Honesto," she explained, passing on small bits of information to stem the tide of more questions from Lillie.

Then she realized her heartbeat had kicked into an up-tempo when she said his name. Could it be the mere mention of Eric caused feelings of pleasure in her...or was it the angst of relationship uneasiness? She wasn't sure, so she tossed both temperaments from her mindset.

"That's good news, Honey. Tell me more when I see you, okay? Oh, and by the way, are you coming up here anytime soon? I've got a special package for you. Three weeks have passed since you've been home. Why don't you bring your new friend along."

"Mom! It is nowhere near the quote, dinner with

my parents' stage, I promise you," she argued.

"Please don't assume anything about what I've told you about him, and no, if I make it up there, I won't be bringing Eric or any other guest. I assure you." She wanted to clear up any questions her mother might've had regarding the man she was happily getting to know.

"I see, Dear. I need to get off this phone anyway; your father is so damned impatient when it comes to shopping trips because of his disdain for being stuck with two women all day long. He's probably pacing the garage right now. And I can predict Doris is ready to get going, too. I might get a drink before shopping with these two characters. Love you, Baby. Bye."

"Bye, Mom. Love you and Dad. And say hello to Aunt Doris for me."

Olivia ended the call and stretched out on the chaise with plans to continue analyzing the data later.

Time slipped by as the afternoon breeze blew across the balcony, and before long, Olivia drifted into a nap. An hour later, she sprang from the comfortable spot. A good portion of her Saturday had already sneaked away.

"I need to finish analyzing these data today. I gotta' get busy. Monday will be here before I know it!" She entered the bedroom from the balcony, locking the sliding glass door. When she walked through her office, Olivia noticed a stack of letters set aside for mailing. Seeing them brought on images of the handsome engineer once more.

Miles away from her, Eric mindlessly watched a college game re-run on the sports channel. The rugged action of the two teams noisily crashing helmets on the large screen was of little interest to him. Instead, his thoughts were on the romantic evening in Long Beach.

Chapter 6
Allegiance

Dr. Reece planned to share details about the London conference with the faculty at Monday's regular meeting. She arrived on campus around 8:00 A.M. to prepare for skeptics like Dan Bledsoe, who'd likely tear into her theoretical paper. He had already objected to Olivia, Kip Thibodeaux and William Gibson representing the university at the prestigious London event. Together, the three would showcase new models in particle physics research to thousands of attendees. High profile sessions like these meant millions in grant funding for the university.

Forty-five-year-old, soft-spoken Kip Thibodeaux was an extraordinary physicist. He was also Olivia's closest faculty ally. Born in Kings County, just south of Fresno and east of Santa Cruz, Dr. Thibodeaux was no stranger to hard work. He'd grown up in a devoutly Catholic middle-class family that shaped his deeply compassionate persona. His father and first role model, Charles Thibodeaux, had worked for many years as a citrus farmer in Southern California.

Striking out on his own, Kip's father, Charles Thibodeaux. disappeared from Baton Rouge right out of high school, wishing to escape the stigma of poverty that attached itself to the Thibodeaux family. He wanted to be done with being poor and couldn't get out of Louisiana fast enough. So he left home never looking back. Charles wanted a better life for himself, and California promised it. But when he reached the Golden State in the mid-eighties, the U.S. was on a slow economic rebound, and few jobs were available.

After a period of dead-end occupations, he was hired to pick oranges in the central California valley and was paid minimum wage. There, he met the love of his life, Angeline. A year after marriage, they started a family, with their first son, Kip. Charles soon landed a job as plant manager with Mancino Family Farms where he remained for forty-one years. The sterling work ethic that Dr. Kip Thibodeaux learned under the guidance of his father, Charles, was evident in his role as a physics instructor. He provided unselfishly to his students, such as giving countless hours toward advising and offering home cooked Cajun meals to anyone who needed that, too. Students flocked to his classes, knowing what they learned would later be priceless knowledge. Dr. Thibodeaux and Olivia collaborated extensively on examining the quantum effects in mechanical systems. Their work gained high international interest.

William Gibson, who reminded others never to call him Bill, received his doctorate from the most prestigious university in New Jersey. He was another of Olivia's trusted allies known for his acclaimed work. He had been recruited aggressively by the Association of Intergalactic Science (AIS) established by NASA but chose to teach, citing his desire to nurture young scientific minds. Despite giving up a dozen invitations to leave the university, Gibson was pursued as an advisor to many of NASA's major projects, including the substation that would later send interstellar communication links to Earth from space.

Recently, Gibson, who'd spent most of his career as a single man, married Emily Woods, a nurse at the regional medical center near UST. Before dating Emily, William's social life outside the university was nonexistent. When not in his office writing passionately on research findings, he spent time at the campus bar pontificating on NASA's extensive list of achievements. Never overbearing to others, his associates happily welcomed his peculiar mad-scientist ranting.

Dr. Gibson's global reputation was also noteworthy. Before joining the UST faculty, he held numerous teaching positions and amassed accolades at venerable universities in Alabama, Massachusetts, and northern California. When Dean Coleman interviewed William for a faculty position, she knew he would be an excellent fit in the department. This year marked his fifteenth year as a full professor.

Faculty relationships in the College of Science was cordial and conflicts rarely occurred. Six women and eight men made up its largest department, which was physics, all bringing superior research and teaching to UST. However, there was one exception - Dr. Bledsoe. At sixty-two years old, the senior physics professor, Dan Bledsoe, was not especially popular amongst his peers. He was best described as a negative-minded iconoclast who was antagonistic toward anything Dean Coleman tried to achieve in the college. In his mind, Bledsoe self-importantly believed he was the indisputable reigning science professor. Bledsoe's haughtiness caused him to believe seniority in the department came with unchecked entitlement, although Dean Coleman had to check his narcissism on far too many occasions. His repellent behavior was caused by resentment of never being promoted to the status of Dean - something he intended when he first arrived at UST. Instead, Dr. Coleman, who'd come one year after him and was five years younger, landed the coveted leadership title. The professor's bitterness for being overlooked never left him. At this time in his career, he appeared to have no intention of ending his mean-spirited attitude toward her. By and large, his only goal was to foment discord.

All the same, Dr. Bledsoe was a deservedly praiseworthy scholar. He was known for numerous international achievements with admirable distinction. His greatest asset to the college was his outstanding abilities in mathematics, by comparing the mathematical consequences of probability data in astrophysics. Bledsoe was published in every reputable physics journal and was known in all scientific circles. But that was where his respected qualities stopped.

Armed with an argumentative attitude, He was known to flaunt his worthiness as a scientist at UST. His spurious behaviors instigated suspicions among peers who believed his only intent was to rip apart and weaken the Dean's administration. Beyond that, he was constantly short tempered and confrontational with anyone who disagreed with him. For certain, he was the only thorn that the Dean had to reckon with in the college. Therefore his behaviors in faculty meetings were routinely and expectedly contentious, as it was soon to be an hour after the meeting started that morning. It all started with Dr. Coleman's praise for the work of Gibson, Reece, and Thibodeaux.

"Dr. Reece, congrats on the London invitation. I want you to know that on behalf of our College, we appreciate you and the exceptional work you've accomplished," the Dean announced in the monthly meeting.

"Thank you, Dr. Coleman," Olivia responded.

"Again, Dr. Reece, Dr. Gibson, and Dr. Thibodeaux, thank you all, for your extraordinary work. The three of you continue to make our university very proud. You've helped us pull in millions for scholarships. That's why your presence in London is so valuable," The Dean lauded them altogether.

"Thank you," they all said.

Bledsoe's irascible nature came through immediately. Wearing an old-fashioned red plaid shirt that confirmed his age, he querulously denounced the idea of having three faculty members at the same conference, pointing out the expense of hotel rooms and airfare to Europe.

Within seconds, Thibodeaux retaliated, "Had it not been for the three of us, the university would not be represented anywhere on the agenda in London next year. Where the hell is your contribution, Dan? I heard your conference proposal was not accepted this time because you're pushing the same old data!"

Contention between Dan and Kip was stirring up again. It was apparent that Kip was not going to retreat from the spiteful and hateful combativeness that expectedly happened between them. Bledsoe's insolent words brought uneasiness among everyone and the stench of his hostility and resentment toward Kip permeated the room.

No one traded looks with either man. Bledsoe's face then turned cardinal red with embarrassment. He reacted in a low monotone,

"There is no cause for you to get upset, Kip. You are going, aren't you?"

"You damn right," Kip gruffly responded.

The tension in the room was strangling. The Dean's eyes darted between Bledsoe and Thibodeaux. Everyone could tell she was about to lose every ounce of composure. But she didn't let the two men get the best of her.

Dr. Coleman's flawlessly tailored pale blue suit, complete with pearls accenting her neck of sagging skin, distinctly set her apart from a room full of subordinates. She was not to be shaken. Her meticulous appearance, including perfectly styled hair and designer glasses, was subtle evidence of her authority as the lead professor in her college. She was, by all accounts, in charge. After teaching physics and earning numerous honors for over twenty-five years, she'd earned her stripes as chief of the science program at UST, and most people respected that. No matter the circumstances, she was always cool and collected, except for now.

Dr. Coleman did not intend to put up with Bledsoe's willful disregard for her leadership. She'd had it with him. A sudden trace of disgust, rarely seen, flashed across the Dean's blushed face. She'd become tired of the unnecessary adolescent behavior between the dueling men. She had no use for such conduct, and their showboating in the middle of meetings needed to cease. The Dean huffed without subtlety. "Okay, guys, there is no need to push this scene any further, especially right now. I'm sure Dan will eventually be published in a known journal and glowing reviews will follow as usual," she hissed with words that were on the edge of contempt.

Dr. Thibodeaux let go of a subdued grumble, smugly folded his thick hairy arms across his chest, and sent a chilling stare toward his half-cocked adversary. Fidgety Bledsoe shuffled in his seat, feigning arrogance and doing everything to dodge Kip's stare. Neither man said anything as they evaded eye contact with everyone else in the room.

The Dean drummed her buff-colored nails, signaling the chilling summit of her irritation.

"Gentlemen, why don't the two of you meet with me in my office at 9:00 A.M next Monday. I expect you both to be there and to be prompt. There's plenty that we have to discuss! Okay, let's end this. In the meantime. I want to thank the rest of you for an otherwise productive meeting today."

Again, pissed with Bledsoe and the way he'd disrupted the meeting, the infuriated Dean stood, waved her hand with disgust and hastily left the room.

Olivia mused, "Next Monday's three-way action in the Dean's office is going to be very, very interesting."

All in all, Olivia was proud of the way Kip handled the crossfire with Dan who often made faculty meetings uncomfortable for others. And even though compassionate and humble, Dr. Thibodeaux would never back down from a self-proclaimed bully like Dan whose personality was every bit distasteful.

Chapter 7
Together

During the weeks following their first date, Olivia was in touch with Eric through text messages and phone calls, often meeting him at Garcia's for lunch. She enjoyed every moment, especially after Long Beach and the memorable dinner at the Moon Eclipse. But her goal was to land a coveted sabbatical in Europe. Dean Coleman had frequently assured her of the Birmingham opportunity in private conversations. The professor's ambitions reminded her that social indulgences had to be minimal at whatever cost, including chances to spend more time with Eric. Nevertheless, there were many times she longed for him and could not erase sweet images of him from her mind.

One Saturday, around noontime, after many hours of working on the London conference presentation, it was time to put her work aside. The previous week ended on a good note. Quiet rumors were that Dr. Coleman was nailing down Dan Bledsoe's nastiness.

Feeling relaxed, Olivia reflected on the amount of work she had accomplished since the crack of dawn; confident that she was close to finalizing her encryption data, she took a well-deserved break. From the balcony, she could see a young family having a good time in their backyard. The afternoon was bathed in sunshine, and the outdoor conditions were unspoiled.

Three small children playfully waved goodbye to a plume of smoke floating above the flaming grill into the clouds. Innocent young laughter and play were heard. Olivia thought of how nice it would be to spend the day with Eric. Minutes later, her phone rang, pulling her away from a comfortable perch on the balcony.

"For the last month, you've been hiding from me. I'm missing you, Olivia Reece."

On the other end of the line, his sexy, half-smile appeared when he declared his loneliness without her.

"I've been snowed under. I'm working hard to get my data summarized," was her answer to his woeful blues.

"Tell me, please," he asked, "when are we going to do something special together again? You know, just like we did in Long Beach? Talking on the phone and having lunch with you at Garcia's once a week has been great, but I want to spend some real time with you again. I want to be alone with you."

The adorable pleading in his voice was hard to resist. By now, she was weakly giving in to the way he made her feel. It was like being kissed by a mind-blowing opiate and she didn't mind getting the inebriating fix.

Although she understood his wishful words, she wanted him to know what the international meeting meant to her and how it would help to advance years of committed research. He, in turn, responded with sincere praise for her achievements.

"Are you doing anything tonight? How about dinner with me?" She asked in a bold flirt, partly inspired by watching the neighbors earlier and because she was beginning to miss him, too. He was flattered and right away accepted her offer, afraid she might change her mind.

"Great. Does seven o'clock sound okay with you?" she asked, overjoyed that he had said yes.

"I'm sure I can make it by then. I'm on my way to meet some of my buddies. Allen Brinks has a sailboat. We drive to the shore one Saturday every month to hang out."

"A sailboat! That's cool. I didn't know engineers were that well off. I ended up in the wrong profession, didn't I?"

"I don't think you did," he charmingly interjected.

"Well, you know what they say about teaching don't you?"

"No. What's that?"

"The cliché is... let's see... they say, 'teaching is a commitment to a lifetime of poverty'. I'm starting to believe that now," she kidded. "A sailboat definitely doesn't fit into my financial plan."

"Let me explain. The sailboat that he owns, with his brother by the way, is tiny, and I emphasize it is a tiny boat." He carefully said each word. "We often wear two life jackets just in case," he remarked jokingly.

"Just in case? Oh, I see," she responded, now more curious. "In case of what?"

"You know, a mishap happening at sea," said Eric, laughing subtly.

"Oh. That doesn't sound too good. You'll have to tell me more about your sailing adventure tonight."

"Sure. Would love to. By the way, can I bring something for dinner? What's your favorite wine?" She adored the sound of his voice. His eloquent, careful articulation and flawless diction were seducing and every word was measured. It was the same kind of assuredness that came across the first day she met him. She could only dream of how much pleasure would come with listening to him all night long. Pleased about his offer to bring wine, she replied, "Thank you. I don't have a wine preference. I like surprises. Please bring whatever you like, Eric."

"It might be a tough assignment, but I'll come up with something," he answered her.

"Okay, I'll see you then." She responded, while no longer bothering to hold back excitement about seeing him soon.

"I'll see you tonight."

When the call ended, Olivia paused and imagined being with him later. She reconnected the phone to the charger. In a flash, she started preparing for the evening.

"What should I do first?" She asked out loud but was quickly cautioned, "Okay, Olivia Reece, chill out now. Don't overthink what's happening here. He's nice and very cute. You've enjoyed hanging out with him so far, but you should wait to see where this goes."

7:00 P.M.

"Hello, Eric."

Olivia looked sensational. She was wearing a flattering blue sun dress that made her look remarkably fit. He stepped back from the doorway nervously admiring her and said, "Hey there, lady. You look so fantastic." He wrapped his arms around her with a gentle hug.

"Thanks," she blushed and returned his embrace.

"Where is the faux Doberman tonight?" he asked. "Is it locked in the garage?" The comment brought a teasing smile and laughter from him, showing he was happy to see her.

"No worries. You can rest knowing he won't be attacking you tonight," said Olivia with a shy smile.

"That's good. I'm feeling much better now."

She pointed him toward the kitchen where she was preparing the meal and offered him a drink.

"Brought wine for us, too," Eric said as he proudly handed her a bottle of Sauvignon Blanc. "Hope you like white wine. The guy at the store showed me ten different bottles before I picked one. I like wine, but I'm no connoisseur; it was a tough assignment for me."

"Thank you. I love this one," she confirmed while examining the label. "Great choice. Now, what would you like - beer, wine, something stronger or softer?"

"That, Madame is a loaded question."

"Why do you say that?"

"I won't say, but in the meanwhile, I'll take a beer. You got any?" She offered him an imported German beer in a familiar green bottle. "That's all I have. Will it do for you?"

"Thanks, I like this one."

"How was today's sailing adventure with your friends?" She questioned him, behind a teasing grin. "Were there any mishaps?"

"None to speak of." He sighed with a smile as his thumb traced the bottle's frosted label.

"What's up? What are you thinking about, Eric?"

"Oh, nothing. Just our day on the water. We had a good time."

"Yes. It was a perfect day wasn't it?" She remembered

watching the children from her balcony. He went on, "And we did a lot of trash-talking about who caught the biggest fish."

"I guess you topped them?" she responded, pouring wine for herself.

"Nah. Not today. Allen got lucky." Still smiling, he sipped the icy beer and watched her remove a white dish from the oven. The mouthwatering aroma made Eric's stomach growl, so he quickly asked forgiveness for seeming eager to eat.

"That smells amazing. What is it?" He asked more about it and why it was special.

"It is a family recipe that came from my great grandmother. The Reece family believes in putting good food on the table."

"My folks are like that, too, but most of all during the holidays. When I'm home at Christmas in Charlotte we enjoy decorating the tree, wrapping gifts, and sharing big meals with lots of food. I always liked that when I was a kid," Eric shared.

"Yeah. I'm sure my Grandma Rachel was sick of fixing this casserole for me, but she never stopped. I hope you like it."

"I'm sure I will."

Earlier in the day, while sailing several miles offshore with his companions, the anticipation of an evening with Olivia had consumed him. Now, he was glad to finally be alone with her, and the occasion, up to that point, was all he'd imagined.

A sensual gaze passed between them when he leaned against the kitchen counter and took another swallow of beer. She couldn't help but notice how the black polo shirt fit him - like a perfectly sized glove. She could see the contour of his broad chest as the rhythm of his breathing stealthily apprehended her.

Being that close to him was just about as hypnotizing as it could possibly get.

"The salad is ready. As soon as the bread is toasted, we can talk more about your day over dinner,"

In that space of time, she needed to say something to shake her fascination with his amazing body.

"The table is already set. For now, make yourself at home." She pointed toward the living room where a large flat-screen TV flashed images of the evening news.

He settled onto the sofa covered with assorted brown, tan, and rust-colored pillows in mixed patterns and textures. He casually stared at the television but thought about how comfortable the room felt and how at ease he was with her. The room was uncluttered. In one corner of the room was a chessboard with hefty marble pieces set up for play.

"I see you play chess." His comment rose above a commercial jingle on the television.

"Yes. My dad taught me the basic strategies. He enjoys chess more than he does golf."

"He did huh?"

"Yes. He once told me that making wise strategic moves in life will lead to success. To me, chess is essentially all of that."

He commented. "Success is all about strategy and persistence, huh?" For Eric, Olivia was unwittingly seducing him with every new thing he learned about her.

"Yes, I agree."

"Tell me, what makes chess different, though?" He was deeply interested in her perspectives on life.

"Not sure of what you're asking. Different from what?"

"I guess I sound like one of your students. I don't know how to phrase the question," he quipped. She was touched by his light humor.

"You're funny."

"It's like checkers, right?" He questioned her sincerely. He'd learned to play checkers like most people growing up in the South: a game that was based on simple strategies.

"Not quite, Eric. Of course, I've only played checkers once or twice. I remember an exercise in a probability class that involved checkers. But chess is actually a lot like military tactics. The object is to threaten to capture the opposing king, or in other words, checkmate your opponent's king."

"Checkmate," he repeated, trying to get to her point.

"I've heard that expression before."

"Yes, The opponent loses as soon as their king is checkmated, sorry to say," she said. He was intrigued by her ability to explain things cleverly. The fellows he knew who played chess would give vague explanations of the game and that made him lose interest. He never bothered to learn. "Would you say it is like doing battle? A war game?"

"Yeah, uh-huh."

"Uh-huh." He echoed her reply and then moved to another topic.

"Your dad taught you well, like how to defend yourself and play chess. What does he do for a living," he asked her, looking at the chessboard and examining the uniquely shaped rook.

"Yes, he's really a great dad. He was the Regional Director of a tech company in Silicon Valley. Five years ago, his early retirement from the company was probably one of his best decisions. Mom retired, too. The company he worked for, *T.S. Brogan Technologies*, mainly focused the 1980s microchip innovations. He was involved in many of the new ideas that came out when he was there," she explained.

"Gotcha'. I've heard of T.S. Brogan." His response was affirming. "What is their angle in today's tech industry?"

"They are based in the Silicon region, but the franchise is in two other locations in the state. Since my dad left, the focus has changed along with new 21st-century innovations. Their latest location is Santa Cruz. That's where he retired from."

"Yeah, some start-up tech companies are opening up there now," he added.

"Because of Dad's business technology credentials, he started working for them as a division manager just out of college. He wanted to get on board with any one of the bigger corporations at that time. But he ended up at T.S. Brogan and actually liked being there, even though it was a much smaller company. My mom worked at a newspaper in the valley for years."

"Which paper was that?"

"The Chronicle. She has a master's. in English and a bachelor's degree in American literature from State U." Olivia went on to say, "Mom always wanted to write more, maybe a novel, but never found the time once she and Dad got together."

"You mentioned your folks live in Santa Cruz. Is that where you're from?"

"No, I was born in Santa Barbara. I was fifteen when we moved to Santa Cruz. Everything about moving there had a big impact on my life."

Her voice lowered as she passed him a corkscrew and took Eric's wine from the fridge.

"Let's eat and enjoy this wonderful wine you brought for us."

While eating, Olivia explained that her parents wanted to travel the globe by taking one international trek each year once they retired. They'd already been to six countries in Europe, four in the Caribbean, and had spent three weeks in South Africa. But it became more difficult to go abroad because of international tension. Their travel plans eventually changed and for Edward Reece, nothing was more important than his family's safety.

Just like the first time Eric's eyes touched her, he was stirred. That evening, the temptation of Olivia seemed infinitely more irrestible than it had ever been. He wanted the evening to last – he was unrushed, savoring every bite and making each mouthful a reason to prolong their time together. He took another plate of pasta, showing that he appreciated her culinary talent. Learning as much as he could about her was his desire.

"I got a better handle on particle physics after we went to Long Beach. So if I ever enroll in your class, I can be prepared."

Appreciably surprised by his interest, she responded, "You did?"

"Yes." His grin was timid and his sincere confession affected her. "Maybe I'll enroll in your class next semester."

"You should. I would love to have you in there."

"By the way, how did you end up in the field of Physics?" he asked, curiously. "

"Believe it or not, I got interested in what I'm researching now when I was in high school. It's been my focus for many years. Luckily, I had a mentor, Dr. Richard Chin. He encouraged me a lot back then. Even now, he reminds me to keep refining my investigative techniques, and... he says before I know it the answers that I'm going after will come."

"That's cool." He wanted to know more. "Is it common for physics scientists to spend as much time on one thing?"

"Absolutely. But that's true for any discipline. It's kinda' like ongoing detective work."

More interested, he asked, "Now, Madame Detective, what is this research you're doing right now?"

"I'm glad you asked," she gleamed. "I have been studying a couple of connective theories over many years now. Trust me though, my efforts are not singular. Others are on the same inquiry trail. But I think what I've done is at the brink of cutting-edge discoveries... but who knows?"

"Tell me more about that."

"A few scientists pursued answers to some of the same theories. I'm aware of at least two well-known physicists who are aggressively chasing the same study as we speak. It is called the Krausberg Effect. According to some, this phenomenon suggests that interstellar technology and aspects of number theory are interconnected. If Krausberg's theory is integrated into this idea, it could change the trajectory of global interactive communication and global navigational devices via satellites. It's pretty remarkable."

Though puzzled, Eric continued to listen.

"Remember, we talked about particle physics on the way to Long Beach? There is a dimension of physics that is still to be uncovered I believe, and I think it will significantly impact us world wide."

He nodded with understanding and a smile.

"You see, I've studied Dr. Krausberg's work and its potential outcomes for nearly half my life."

He reacted, "That sounds pretty complicated."

"Yes, I suppose most people would agree with you; but if you think about it, it's really not that complex," she answered animatedly.

"Here is why. Dr. Krausberg was a German physicist, who in the early 1900s, contributed generously to the foundations in the concept of intra-quantum refractions of the electromagnetic field," she maintained.

"Oh? Sounds cool, but I don't know what that means." He was perplexed, yet he marveled at the way she explained things.

Recognizing that her theories rarely found an audience outside academic gatherings, Olivia excitedly divulged her role in science. She went on., sparing him the details that only physicists would understand. "

"As this relates to my interest in particle physics, these intra-quantum refractions are microscopic, and in most normal cases, they'd never be noticed. This research is being used in the development of an interstellar substation model because those tiny particles can store massive amounts of data that can be protected in the substation, in a place away from easy access. The substation is projected to house billions of nano-communication chips, shall we say, perhaps like the size of the dust on your dashboard. In the substation, they will be protected from nefarious adversaries."

As they cleared the dinner table, she continued to explain her theory with everyday relatable examples.

"Of course today, someone smart enough can possibly tap into the satellite navigational space from any place on the globe –maybe from a perpetrator's home-office or their kitchen table - and commence to alter, or shall we say, screw up pretty much all of our institutions - from political to financial. That is why there is greater concern about the manipulative powers of outside influences and how they might negatively intervene. But mind you, even after all these years, we're still working on strong competing theories about this. That's just how science works."

"I wanna' know more about your research sometime."

"Okay. Glad to tell you what I have learned."

Shortly afterward, they ended up in the livingroom with another glass of wine.

"It is too bad you don't play chess," she said, sitting close by and drawing on his hypnotic essence.

"No, I don't. I would love to learn though. I'd probably do better at understanding chess than learning about your Krausberg research. Will you teach me to play chess?"

He stared into brown eyes that sparkled back when an outpouring of bottomless desire took hold of him.

Returning his gaze, she answered, "Of course I will."

"I'd like to learn the game," he repeated.

"Okay. I think you could be quite good at it. Maybe the next time you're here we'll try your hand at a game or two."

"Yeah, I like the idea of the next time, and... the next time... and the next...," he spoke softly, reaching for her hand.

His gentle touch was inducing, clouding all of her senses. She welcomed him. Affectionate touching was passed back to him as he pulled her closer for the kiss she'd dreamed of all day. She succumbed and surrendered to his masculinity, which was gently syncing with her feminine desires. The sweetness of Olivia's lips unleashed passion that had not been ignited in him for some time. It was an emotion of which he'd been robbed. Two years had ebbed away since he'd held a woman with so much desire. What he was experiencing at that time with her was indescribable. And like nothing else, his yearnings and sensations were heightened by her touch.

Neither of them could deny what they were feeling, because their urges were no longer tempered by hesitation. And neither of them cared.

She led him to her bedroom, knowing by now there was no turning back. Together, the couple wrestled in the dark to drop a shirt, trousers, and sundress to the floor, and in that time, finding affectionate humor between tender, playful kisses. They touchingly mocked each other's clumsiness and before long were folded into each other. He whispered hoarsely, "I've been longing for this time with you, Olivia. But if you think we shouldn't, we don't have to."

"It's alright. I've been waiting for you, too," she breathed, nestled on the bed and waiting for another kiss.

Sensual tension unfolded when his mouth explored all of her. He kissed her silken neck, kissing all the way down to her soft delicate feet. The bedroom was flooded with an erotically sweet mixture of Olivia's perfume on her soft skin, and his insatiably hungry desire to love her.

Her lover's advances were rough, then gentle, then rough again, causing the headboard of the king-sized bed to bump the wall in the thumping rhythm of their sweaty, coupled bodies. The tapping and bumping lulled her closer to the man who was passionately suffusing her with his abandoned, unrestrained love.

During the whole time, her fingers roughly stroked his back as a sign of her satisfaction, all the while wanting more of him in the darkness. Later, they lingered together for another hour before he left.

Sunlight seeped through the windows in Eric's bedroom the following morning. He slid from under the covers and strolled across the cool floor toward the shower.

Half-asleep and peering at his reflection in the mirror, he winked at the image staring back at him and smilingly approved. He'd slept well. His first thoughts were of Olivia and how much he had enjoyed being with her the night before. His face released a grateful smile when he turned his back to the mirror to see red marks as evidence of their lovemaking. He remembered holding and loving her and how she willingly gave herself to him. Something was developing between them, and to his joy, it felt right.

Later in the day, he called and thanked her for dinner but also apologized if his moves had been out of bounds.

"I hope you're not regretting being with me last night."

She answered, "I woke up to thoughts of you this morning, Eric. I'm really glad you came over."

She then said, "I'll be thinking of you today. I'm leaving in a little while to see my folks in Santa Cruz. I won't return before tomorrow afternoon."

Eric penned a letter to her, recalling their first night of complete, physical intimacy.

Olivia,

In the short time that we have known each other, you've given me more joy than I've ever experienced with another; and for that, I am thankful. I will do any and everything to make you happy. I will do so because I want to experience real love with you, and only you, forever. What more could a man want? I'm lucky to have met you. Eric

After the painful breakup with Jasmine, he wanted to protect his heart and was afraid that the ghosts of a past relationship might find him once again. The love letter to Olivia was ripped up and thrown away.

Chapter 8
Changes

An anxiously awaited autumn began to creep into California, occasionally hiding between hot and balmy days that hung over the city like an unwanted, heavy veil. San Honestans retreated to places like Garcia's for libatious refuge. Even so, the slow approach to summer's end didn't change the UST tempo that was bustling with students and faculty on campus.

"Good morning, Ms. Marshall. What's going on?" Ms. Marshall had hurriedly entered Olivia's office and closed the door. Her concerned expression was telling.

"Dr. Reece, I want to give you the latest on something that's going on. Do you have a minute?"

"Sure, I have a little time before my class starts. What's up?"

Olivia stopped reviewing the iPad notes, pushed the device to an empty spot on the desk, and turned toward the woman whose olive skin kept secrets about her middle age. Even though hot pink lipstick didn't enhance the woman's features, she wore it daily. .

"Dr. Coleman is planning to persuade Dr. Bledsoe to retire this year. I think she's had it with his rudeness and criticisms."

"What?" Olivia asked, apparently thrown.

"I didn't tell anyone else yet, Doc. It's supposed to be kept quiet until she talks to him in a couple of days, but I wanted to let you in on it early."

Ms. Marshall's breaking news was pushed down to a

muffle inside the walls of Dr. Reece's office. It was a major turning point for a faculty beleaguered by Bledsoe's actions. Although Ms. Marshall was speaking cautiously, she trusted Olivia and was at ease sharing 'classified' information with her. Dr. Reece was often the first to know about departmental decisions due to her friendship with Ms. Marshall. Their talks were, as they promised each other, confidential.

"What happened?"

"She asked me to prepare a letter telling him she'll recommend him as the next UST Physics Emerita. That is, after completing this contract year. And that she'd be honored if he decided to accept it." Ms. Marshall gestured quotation marks with her fingers as she said emerita. She waited for a reaction from the puzzled professor.

Olivia took quick sips of mint tea before speaking. "My goodness, Ms. Marshall. That's a clever move by Dean Coleman. But do you think there's going to be a backlash from Dan? He'll probably raise hell to the Union."

"Dr. Coleman is being careful not to cross any legal boundaries by avoiding a demand for him to retire. You know how Dr. Bledsoe is. I've heard he drinks a lot, too. But that's just a rumor, you know. Who knows what he will do. I just hope this situation ends without a lot of drama."

Olivia shot a cautious reaction to Ms. Marshall's comments. "I don't like to speculate about people's drinking habits. It's not my business, and carrying on such talk is counterproductive. I only hope there are no volatile repercussions from her decision."

Dr. Reece recalled Bledsoe's attempts to undermine Kip Thibodeaux and others in the department. In past contentious encounters with coworkers, mulish Bledsoe had been every bit vindictive.

Later in the Day at 2:15 P. M., a call from Eric was a much-needed diversion from Olivia's frenzied day.

"Hey there. Gotta' quick question for you. Brinks and Shannon are going up to Redwood National Park for the Labor Day holiday. Would you be interested in going along with us… to be my weekend date… maybe?"

He hesitated at the last words because he didn't want her to think he was making disrespectful assumptions about their past intimacy.

"I'd like to go up north with you guys. Thanks for asking me."

"Cool." He responded casually.

"Classes are suspended Friday because of the holiday. It works for me."

As they talked, she felt a greater sense of trust. And why not travel with him? She liked him.

"I'll call you tonight with details about the trip," he promised.

Eric pressed the off button on his phone and sucked in an easy, relaxed breath. He was feeling satisfied that his relationship with Olivia was deepening. It meant plenty to know that she regarded him in such a way.

After ending the conversation with Olivia, he called Allen to confirm that their weekend plans were set. As he waited for Allen to answer, his thoughts turned to his past. All too well, he knew the pain of love and the pure hell of a nasty breakup. The split with Jasmine had been a stinging, telling experience. The way she had abused his emotions and unhinged his heart damaged his perceptions of women and the purity of love.

A few years before meeting Olivia Reece, he naively fell for Jasmine, wanting her to be a lifetime soulmate. Instead, Jasmine forced him to deal with a spate of jealous accusations, frequent arguments, constant distrust, and the wrath of untoward actions that later caused him to avoid dating altogether. Everything he recalled about his former girlfriend was sadly disappointing, to the extent that he blocked any thoughts of ever being in love with her.

By contrast, Olivia was changing his ideas on love. Maybe she would be the one to help him finally break from his animosity about romance. Quite possibly he could erase the failure of empty promises that plagued his emotionally broken past.

There were more signs that Olivia had genuine care for him. He also believed there was something special in how they connected when their bodies were entwined, dancing in sweet, unabridged rhythm.

He often thought of the first night of making love with her and recalled the throaty murmurs of evocative pleasure that made him thankful she was responding to the love he felt.

Eric's daydream abruptly stopped when Allen Brinks

finally answered his call. Once a few hotel reservation details were discussed, the Labor Day trip was confirmed.

7:30 A.M. Early morning brought with it an air of tranquility in San Honesta. In every part of the city, residents were waking to an uncommonly cool sixty-four degrees on a Labor Day weekend. It was an anomalous cold snap for a place that yeilded high temperatures. A stunning dawn inspired even late morning sleepers to rise early. For some, resisting such a picturesque day would have been sacrilege.

Delvin Place Community (DPC, a San Honesto neighborhood where Allen Brinks and his fiancé, Shannon, lived), was an upscale, ultra-hip revitalized community for up-and-coming professionals. The diverse population appealed to young lawyers, geeky tech developers, social media entrepreneurs, non-profit development officers, and aspiring mid-level managers in public service arenas. It was a compelling attraction to a beautiful mosaic of ethnicities and racial groups.

Most of the Delvin Place residents were Millenials who enjoyed working in the high technology, cyber-driven world of interactive platforms. Notably, this generation was rapidly moving away from old methods of tactile engagement toward new business relations that required less human interaction. Essentially, Millennials controlled the tech-driven arena because, by far, they created it.

The quaint development was fertile ground for exploring nanotech optics communication. Funds jointly contributed by the City of San Honesta and UST in the amount of well over two-point-five million dollars for infrastructure spending were line-itemed and allocated to the neighborhood specifically for that purpose. This area in San Honesto also boasted an active nightlife where residents could attend trendy gatherings, and at the same time, build business partnerships. A main goal of the Delivn Place community was to have less vehicular presence and more green-space. It was a concept that was changing how social engagements and business happened. Replications of this residential model were popping up along the West Coast, as well as in Chicago, Boston, Charlotte, and many cities in the Midwest and East.

Even though people moved to the Delvin Place Community (DPC) for different reasons, it was clear that many came there because the niche had a unique generational identity with a highly energized and vibrant pulse. Moreover, the community was quickly distinguishing itself from densely populated urban centers that were becoming anachronisms.

In the last three years, because of the growth explosion, real estate developers were reaping financial rewards by fulfilling the demands made by new homeowners and ambitious investors alike in DPC. San Honesto leaders, in response, dedicated a good portion of their budget to upgrading streets, sidewalks, and public transportation services in the subdivision. Like so many other neighborhoods where demands of environmental protection and innovative green lifestyles were in vogue, the subdivision quickly became a popular hub for its millennial trendsetters.

It was also in Delvin Place, where homes that were built five decades before were transformed into cottage-styled, garden-scaped residences with modern features that made life stress-free. Allen Brinks had already moved into the neighborhood and taken advantage of the revitalization incentives after purchasing and renovating a moderate-sized two-bedroom bungalow on Rosenwald Street. It was at Allen's house on Rosenwald from where the two couples departed for the Redwoods trip north.

On the road to Redwood State Park, the couples bonded quickly, as had been predicted. Olivia admired Allen and Shannon's relationship, which reminded her of the intimate times she shared with Eric. There was a certain kind of comfort developing in the relationship with Eric, and Olivia welcomed the closeness that made her feel safe and desired by him. In truth, he'd already stolen her heart.

The drive was many hours long, but soon, the foursome reached the hotel at the edge of the Eel River. The couples were amazed by the forested grounds and lush landscape. A mammoth fountain spewed tons of water high above exotic foliage. It was a lush setting in the forested hideaway. By the time they reached the hotel and checked in, they were ready for a good meal and a comfortable bed.

From the suite window, Olivia marveled at the panoramic view overlooking a river that traced along a breathtaking forest around the property. Massive trees stood guard over the well-turned resort, where she relished the ball of orange sun that slowly descended behind a wall of Sequoias. Right then, the unspoiled moment caused her to reflect upon what life had given her and what life was also promising with a man she hesitantly began to love.

He hugged Olivia as she pressed herself onto his chest. Every second near him was potent. He whispered, "I need you, Olivia,"

That night, they tasted the sweet flavors of an evolving love. Neither space nor air could find its way between them, with strong hands clutching and tiny hands squeezing; he was tethered by her passion, and she by his. The unbound expressions of love were reciprocated by another, then another, to each other. When the licentious entanglement ended, Olivia fell asleep in Eric's arms. As he held her, he saw an enviably satisfied woman he wanted to love forever. Her slumber gave him a chance to savor her extraordinary beauty gratefully and to take pleasure in their satisfying lovemaking. As an affirmation of his deepening love, her sleeping body gently shifted in response to his caress. He pulled her nearer in thankfulness and fell asleep.

Days after, back at home from the trip, Eric wrote to Olivia about his feelings. Although, hesitant to express his sentiments in writing, he felt compelled to do so.

Olivia, I dream of one day watching a movie at home with you curled up beside me, eating popcorn and sipping a glass of bourbon. You are my love, Olivia, and my love is deepening unconditionally. Nothing else matters. Happiness is the ultimate consequence of our love for each other. Eric

Three weeks later, a Saturday night for Olivia turned into an early Sunday morning in Eric's arms. She was comfortable staying the night with him after going on the Redwood Forest Labor Day trip. She overlooked the need to go home because she was falling in love, and it was soothing to feel his touch in the middle of the night.

That morning, water swashing against the frosted glass in his shower awakened her. There was no surprise to find him out of bed at that hour since rising before dawn was his habit. She listened to his cheerful baritone voice as he hummed a tune from the movie they'd watched the night before.

The shower door slammed shut, and she pictured hot water and mounds of lathery soap on every inch of him. In her mind's eye, she could see a tight abdomen, set off with strong quads that supported Eric's perfectly carved frame. He was the man she adored without repent. She lay there minutes longer and listened, clothed in nothing but his cologne-scented t-shirt.

"I want to be near him," she thought.

Pushing the covers aside, she swung her legs around and let them dangle to the floor. Bare feet with bright red nail polish sank into the thick, white rug next to the bed. Lifting his shirt above her head, she tossed it aside, pulled tangled hair from her face, and tiptoed across the room toward his singing.

Although the bedroom remained dark, a tiny light peeked beneath the bathroom door. Olivia turned the doorknob and sneakily entered the steamy room. Through the frosted shower glass door, she saw beautiful brown skin, enhanced by soapy water rushing downward, touching the curves on his back along the path of a strong spine, over muscular legs. She was longing to share the wet and misty space with him. She quietly tipped to the shower door as he continued to sing. The stall was clouded in a voluminously vaporous fog. She stepped inside and circled her arms about him from behind.

"Good Morning." She was gripped with the pleasure of touching him.

Warmly surprised, he reacted, "Morning, Beautiful. I thought you were asleep. I didn't want to disturb you, especially after last night." His teasing confession came from a face covered with bubbly, white lather.

"Last night? What happened?"she asked, pretending to be confused.

"Huh? You don't know?"

"I don't remember anything except the movie, some whiskey, and way too much pizza," she giggled.

"Well, Dr. Reece, let me help you recall the details," as he turned his effervesced physique to her. His kiss touched the tip of her nose and this evoked memories of what they had enjoyed in his bed hours before. She responded to his affection by standing on her toes to seal her lips with his. The kiss was bitterly soapy yet deliciously pleasing. The couple embraced in a five-by-six-foot space of steaminess with no room between them, melding into one another.

Streams of water shot from the copper showerhead in rapid bursts, covering them in delicious passion. The touch of his chest against her churned the love they shared as she hugged him tightly to taste every bit of his affection. There was nothing he wanted to do other than satisfy her. She opened up to his desire to please her, and all the while giving pleasure back to him.

Fulfilled with his attentive lovemaking, she felicitously confided love for him through intimate eyes and said, "Eric, it's all coming back to me now. Yes, I think I do remember what happened last night."

She knew then she was becoming comfortable with Eric in her life. Something inside her was craving more of him that made her feel safe and needed as she surrendered to their evolving relationship. She desired his constant, unadulterated care. The fusion of his love and her desire to be loved was far better than anything she'd ever experienced.

Chapter 9
Confession

On a mid-November evening, Olivia stopped by Eric's place with exciting news. A gushing smile marked her face. There was something she wanted to share, and she couldn't wait to tell him about it. When she flipped her oversized purse onto the couch, it toppled his flight training manual filled with neatly scribbled notes and cockpit diagrams to the floor. He'd spent the afternoon studying for a much-anticipated and known to be rigorous pilot's examination.

"Guess what, Babe!" She was bubbling over. Unable to answer at once, he sat with arms folded, now baffled by her overly cheerful mood. She could hardly contain herself as she ran across the room, straddled his lap, and kissed him tenderly. "Guess what!" she excitedly repeated.

"What's going on?" He asked, searching for answers in her sparkling brown eyes.

"I got it!" she shrieked. "I got it, Eric!"

"What are you talking about? What did you get?"

"The sabbatical! They gave it to me! I'm going to Birmingham, England. I'll be gone for eight months!" She released a deafening scream.

"Okaaay… Okaaay?" The words spilled from him like thick molasses as he slowly processed the riveting words pouring from her. For a moment, he didn't respond to the announcement. On the contrary, she was exuberant and visibly psyched. Oblivious to Eric's confusion, she went on with details of the exciting news.

"I am so happy! Do you remember Dan Bledsoe?"

"Yeah," he answered, vaguely remembering the professor who made life miserable for everyone in the physics department. "Well, Dan Bledsoe's invitation to leave the department offered by Dean Coleman... or some believed, required retirement, shifted research sabbaticals for everyone, including the one for me!"

"What does that have to do with you, Olivia?" He needed a better idea of what she was disclosing for the first time.

"Today, Dean Coleman emailed her decision to grant me eight months in Europe. I was shooting for six months of research there - at least part of a semester, you know?"

"Okaaay," he said again.

"But Dean Coleman decided that the years I've put into my research justified more time there."

He, still puzzled, let go of one more, "Okaaay?"

She excitedly said, "And when I spoke with the Dean, she clarified that the London conference also prompted the Birmingham decision. It was a no-brainer. Am I lucky or what!"

He was put off guard, now reeling from what he'd just heard. He couldn't speak. Somehow, her disturbing revelation caused a deluge of hurt and confusion to drown him.

"Aren't you happy for me?" She asked, apprehensively.

"I am, Sweetie. No one deserves a chance like this more than you. You've worked so hard for it; what you're doing will be history-making. I'm sure of it, Olivia."

"Well then what's wrong, Eric? Tell me, please, what's wrong?" She sincerely pleaded for an answer.

"I have to get over the shock. The thought of you leaving the country for so long is tough to swallow."

He was attempting a weak shadow of a smile that pushed the corners of his lips downward. He looked away from Olivia's probing eyes because he didn't want her to see his apparent disappointment. Her excitement was suddenly cut short.

"I've talked about this opportunity with you before. You shouldn't be taken aback."

Hoping to get an explanation of his seemingly distressed state, she waited for him to say something, but nothing else came forth.

"I'm going to England for eight months. I should take this opportunity because I may never get it again. I couldn't possibly say no to Dean Coleman's generous permission, and I hope you support that."

"I completely support you, Babe. You're right and I'm happy for you. But I'll miss you when you're away, that's all,"

She said, "You mean the world to me. In the last several months, our bond hasn't been measured by the times we've made love together; it's more than that. No one else makes me happier than you. No one else."

He returned a smile at hearing the pureness of her words. It took everything in him to hold back from expressing his anguish. He continued to listen.

"Honestly, Eric. Only you have helped me appreciate my quirkiness or my silly imperfections. You've helped me understand that it's okay to be me and not have to apologize to anyone. Through you, I've come to know that the mistakes I've made or will make later in life are just that – mistakes. And you've reminded me that understanding and fixing mistakes can make you a better person."

She paused while noticing glimmers of dejection cast upon an otherwise handsome face. She confessed more.

"You've helped me appreciate the beauty of friendship; you've shown me how important it is to build good relationships with anyone in my life. I am glad and blessed because you're in my life, Eric."

"And you in mine," he said.

Into her tearful eyes, he looked, hoping she could see the sadness in him. "I love you so much, Olivia."

Later, they went to bed with no more talk of her news.

In the morning, just before daybreak, he started a fresh pot of coffee and quietly slid back into bed. In the stillness, the glow of sunlight filtered through the bedroom blinds and artfully tagged the furniture with playful, mysteriously shaped silhouettes. Her peaceful, rhythmic breathing occasionally broke the silence, which was in stark contrast to his suffocating worries. While staring at the ceiling, his memory returned to the night before. Her decision to accept the sabbatical was abysmally wounding. His mind was racing out of control as he thought of Olivia's plans to go to Europe. He couldn't understand why his fears were being ruled by what she told him. Still brooding, he turned his back to her, hoping to brush from his mind all of what he'd learned.

By mid-morning, the aroma of coffee invaded her subconsciousness. She burrowed under the sheets, not yet ready to get up. Making love with him the previous night had exceeded all times before. Admittedly, the sum of his intimacy always seemed to linger with her, but this morning, it stayed, clinging to her so much longer than usual.

When she sat up in bed with knees drawn to her chest, she was puzzled to see him sitting across the room in the oversized chair. He was reserved, and his truculent disposition sparked concern.

"Good morning." She roughly rubbed her eyes to remove the last residue of sleep. There was a hint of early morning daylight, but the shadows in the room bore no signs of what the coming day would bring.

"Morning. Here's coffee for you." He limply held the cup in her direction and deliberately avoided her inquiring eyes. As much as he wanted to conceal his state of mind, he failed. He couldn't look directly at her.

"Thanks. It smells wonderful. I'm ready for a cup. How are you feeling today?" She wanted to know before accepting his offer of coffee. She propped her back on a mound of pillows, waiting for his reply.

"I'm good. I'm good," he repeated.

She curiously tilted her head toward his troubled face to see what was different in him. His changed demeanor from the way they had made carnal love was strangely out of character. On any other day, he would have been challenging her to an early morning power walk or playfully chasing her for more of the hot love they'd enjoyed in the midnight hour.

Rather, he seemed oddly distant. His attitude had shifted. "Let me make breakfast for you," she offered, attempting to diminish the rising wall of uneasiness in the room.

"How about eggs, bacon, and some fresh fruit?"

"Uh-huh. Yeah. Yes. Thanks."

"Is something bothering you?" she asked while sorting through her mind for what might have triggered his sour mood.

His outstretched arm held the coffee cup in her direction as he spoke. "Alright? I guess it will be. I guess it will be," he shrugged. It was rare that he repeated himself that way and whenever he did his emotions churned.

Eric's salty behavior incensed her. All at once, disbelief about the way he was acting soared up in her.

"Okay, Mr. Blake, let's talk. It looks like there is a huge... ass... elephant... in the room that needs slaying."

Without the slightest warning, his scathing attitude was fully unmasked, and his angry words climbed three decibels. "Damn, Olivia! We've started something! I thought we were about to change our lives together, but then this happened!"

At the onset of the angered exchange with her, his muscular body stiffened, and the prominent lines on his face were apparent. His frustration was aimed at her. He slammed both cups of coffee onto the nightstand. One cup splashed hot liquid onto the tiled floor, creating a brown stain in the middle of the imported white rug.

"Let me try this once more. What, Mr. Eric Blake, are you referring to?" She asked in disbelief, raising her eyebrows and tilting her head to get a better look at his face in the shadowy bedroom. His anger popped.

"This, sudden departure! This, I must go to England

decision of yours! This decision to go to England without giving me any kind of forewarning! Don't you think your actions are unfair? Don't you!" He was flinging every pain struck word at her.

Olivia's frame of mind instantly changed. His needy, childish outburst confounded her. For the first time, she was witnessing another inexplicable side of him. "Where's this attitude coming from?" She wondered silently as she watched him pace the room.

Everything that happened then turned into flashbacks of turbulent times with her ex, David, who would go into disputations about his self-absorbed life and what he needed in a woman. A woman whom he presumed would abdicate independence when in a serious relationship.

When with David, she refused to hand her free will over to him just because he was her boyfriend. No damn way! And she was not about to give in to Eric either, no matter how much she loved him! To have this happening to her once again was utterly absurd!

Burning up with anger, she slid from the covers. Her nakedness, at that time, mattered to neither of them. She quickly gathered her lingerie', which had been strewn about the room the night before....much like a trail of breadcrumbs to the bed.

As if in the scene of a gripping cinema, Olivia's nude frame moved like that of an agitated lion while she pulled on her blouse and jeans. Dramatically, she flung a thick bed pillow to the floor in resentment of the vitriolic moment. It was the easiest way of showing how upset she was about his bizarre behavior. Throwing something directly at him in that instance would have been a downright contradiction of her consistently poised character. He crossed the room and sat down. Now appearing more distraught and helpless, he watched from the giant velvety chair, increasingly unsure of what to say. For a split second, he started to speak but stayed quiet because he didn't want to ignite Olivia's anger any further.

She fired off, "I don't know which part of I love you, you do not understand, Eric, but I do love you!"

Shaking her head and jabbing her finger in his direction, she angrily went on to say. "Before I met you, I was happily digging into my career and finding satisfaction. I wasn't searching for someone like you. I wasn't searching for anyone, but you showed up unexpectedly. You showed up in the most mind-blowing, most beautiful way! And Eric, I have loved every minute of what we've had so far. But dammit, I must find my happiness, too; just like you are seeking yours. Pretty soon, you'll get your pilot's license. That is something you've longed for!"

She kept talking as she fumbled through the nightstand clutter for her watch and earrings.

"Why are you behaving like this toward me? Your becoming a pilot is so damned wonderful! I'm happy for you. Every bit of your happiness means as much to me as it does to you, goddammit, Eric! Don't you get that!"

He said nothing. His eyes cautiously studied her enraged face, but he could not verbalize what he was going through in that combative moment. He dropped his head and stared at the floor...motionless. Her reaction bitterly stung every part of him.

"If it is okay with you, Mr. Blake, let's talk later today or tomorrow. I am available to do so if you'd like to have a mature, adult conversation about this. But right now, we both need some thinking space between us. I should get out of here!"

With her emotions in flames, she rushed from the room, leaving him drowning in confusion. It was not how he hoped the discussion would go, although he wanted to talk about what was troubling him. Crushed, he feared the possible end of something meaningful with someone he cared so much for. How could this be happening when, just days ago, their lives were inseparable? A mood of blue overwhelmed him. A mood of unbearable sadness covered him as he heard her black coupe recklessly speeding out of the driveway.

He wiped the spilled liquid from the floor and adjusted the two cups of coffee on the nightstand with plans to empty them later. But at that point, he just wanted to soothe his aching heart. So he stretched himself across the bed and contemplated his next move.

He couldn't rid himself of the tight wrench of anxiety squeezing his soul. What just occurred badly wounded him and he struggled to find meaning in what she'd said. In that troubled instance, everything about the relationship was absent of reasonable clarity.

"I love her. I never dreamed I'd love anyone this way but I do love her... Damn, damn, damn."

The drive home for Olivia was exhausting, and the Veteran's Day weekend traffic added to her mounting frustrations. The exit was still two miles ahead, and she would be jailed in slow-moving traffic for at least a half hour or more with others helplessly trapped on the crowded roadway. "Goddammit, Eric Blake!" She screamed loudly as if he were sitting next to her. "Who do you think you are? Who the hell do you think I am? His behavior is crazy! It is absolutely insane!" Her eyes welled with tears that dampened her face and seeped into her aching heart. She remembered every detail of the raging talk she'd just had with the man she loved. His rambling, incoherent sermon mystified her. Even with all of her experience as a scientist, she had no answers for his bizarre actions.

Why did going after her dreams compel so much worry in him? In her view, their relationship was diaphanous. Was it as transparently honest as she hoped? By all accounts, she was officially his girlfriend and his only bed partner, at least as she could tell. But until then, no commitments or abiding promises had ever been proclaimed out loud – most likely because they both withstood tumultuous pasts.

Their mutual affections were no mystery and the relationship was becoming decidedly exclusive. Olivia had no interest whatsoever in anyone else, and all indications suggested that he felt the same way about her. Why then was he behaving as if being away from each other for a short time would be a crisis? His out-of-the-blue meltdown was a shock.

She was hurting from the sharpness of Eric's piercing words. Based on what they'd experienced together in the past months, this abrupt change of attitude was uncharacteristic and at that juncture, she was uncertain as to how she would deal with it.

Arriving home, she waved at the security guard clearing visitors that entered the private neighborhood. He returned the greeting, recognizing her as she drove by. Satisfied that she didn't have to punch in her gate code, she rushed to her place.

Hurrying into the kitchen, she wanted to unload her frustrations onto someone she could trust. At first, she dialed her mother but canceled the call. She needed to have a face-to-face talk with Lora. Using her iPad, she decided to Facetime her best friend.

Lora frowned concernedly and examined her girlfriend's troubled face on the screen.

"Hey. What's wrong?" she asked Olivia, whose vermillion eyes were puffy from flooding tears.

"Can you tell I'm upset?" Olivia tearfully replied.

"Oh yes. I can see the steam sprouting from your ears, Dr. Reece. Spill it."

"Lora, I don't get it. What in the world is happening with this crazy, stupid love affair that I'm going through?"

"What is going on, Olivia?"

There was an urgency to let go of the emotional outrage, and she knew that Lora's raw and candid opinions of her troubles would set her on the right path. With Lora's help, shedding and unmasking her feelings was always comforting.

"We had a bad argument and then it turned into a fight. Why is this happening between us? He was throwing a damn tantrum!"

"Hold on. Who fought? You and Eric?"

"Yes, I guess you can say it is our first argument. We

both said hurtful things to each other, harsh words that neither of us could take back. I screamed some things that were probably unfair, too."

"Oh?" Lora asked.

"He shouted some mean things at me. He was so pitiful when I told him about my sabbatical. It was as if it were the end of the world for him, Lora!"

"Look, whether you've realized it or not, the two of you have forged a beautiful bond. I've noticed it. I'm sure others have, too. And everyone else can see how you've begun to change, Olivia. You seem so much happier. You know... more content."

"Why didn't I see this coming?"

"I don't understand. Are you talking about love? Girl, please. What planet have you been orbiting, Ms. physics professor?"

Lora's comedic response eased Olivia's worries. Her friend was good at deciphering the worst scenarios. So it was a mystery why Lora, who dated regularly, had not enjoyed authentic romance before finally dating Keith.

"Okay," Olivia conceded. I got ya'."

"You do love Eric. You know that don't you? It is evident by your actions and the way you speak of him. Your eyes get dreamy; you smile at the mention of his name, and you include him in practically every part of your life without ever thinking about it."

"Humm. You may be right."

"I may be right? No, Olivia Reece, I know I'm absolutely right."

"Okay, Lora."

"You have every reason to be upset about the way he reacted, but my suggestion is that you mend this silly rift, and I mean pronto. You're a lovely couple and are right for each other." Lora said, "Remember the reception your college hosted a while back? He made it clear to everyone that the both of you were together."

Olivia smiled, thinking of the well-attended affair held in the campus ballroom. That evening, she'd introduced her date to coworkers as she advocated funding to bolster the scholarship program for deserving students. She was relaxed with Eric near her when they mingled with potential donors. He, in turn, marveled as she talked with others, proving her giftedness in science.

Lora interrupted Olivia's silent recollection of the reception and asked, "What is the problem? You two love each other. Why are you behaving like a love-struck teen?"

Ignoring Lora's taunt, she announced, "You should have seen him acting like a darn two-year-old when I was with him this morning!" She shook her head and recalled what happened. She was still baffled by his testy attitude.

"It could be you're lodged in a pitiful state because you will be gone away for such a long time," Lora reminded her.

Trying to hide her fragile feelings, Olivia uttered, "Lora, you are way too logical for me."

With a subtle, restrained laugh that showed concern for her best friend's state of mind, Lora suggested, "Reach out to your man and tell him how much you care. Tell him whatever is necessary to make it alright with you two. But make sure he understands your career is important to you, especially the sabbatical. I know you can work this out. When you leave for

England, you want him to be waiting for you when you return, don't you? No one else is right for you, Olivia. No one. I believe that." she explained.

"Maybe you're right. Gotta let go of this immature anger that I'm feeling right now, and I hope he will let go of his, too."

"Yes," Lora agreed.

"Okay, I am going to call him this afternoon. I'll go back to his place to talk with him. I do care and I'd be a mess without him." She thanked her girlfriend for the sensible advice, who pointed out that her thanks was not necessary.

"I will let you know how it goes," she said, ending with a good-bye.

"I'm here for you if you need me," Olivia's friend emphasized. "Oh, and one more thing, congrats. You deserve the chance to go to England. I'll miss you, but Keith and I are very happy for you."

Later that day, he was in her doorway with his hands shoved deep in his pockets; the slouchy jeans and baggy shirt conveyed how much he was hurting. His face looked worn as if he'd missed hours of rest. With pleading eyes and eyebrows arched upward in pursuit of forgiveness, he searched for signs of love in her saddened face. She was glad to see him and eager to reciprocate his apology. She let him in. Because of his unceasing love, he'd asked if they could talk and sort things out. He wanted them to get past the touchy argument that happened hours before. She, in turn, responded to his offer of love, having desires to mend the hurt feelings and to say goodbye to their differences. They were beginning to realize how genuine love was supposed to feel. Both apologized and held each other close. During those forgiving hours, they promised never to harbor such anger again.

Chapter 10
Declaration

The meeting in late November, between Velocity and Ergowilst in Sacramento, ended in the afternoon. Allen and Eric hurried to get on the road to San Honesto, hoping to get home before nightfall. Allen, who was behind the wheel of the rented sedan, maneuvered around cars racing above the speed limit on Interstate 5. Meanwhile, the hours-long meeting ran through Eric's mind.

He recalled how odd it was that Lukas asked so many questions about Olivia's work concerning the substation. Eric had mentioned the project a few times offhandedly to people he knew, but no details of her work had risen in conversation with Lukas to any great extent. This time though, Lukas asked for specifics, more than that which Eric knew of Olivia's involvement in the project. Though puzzled by Lukas' sudden interest, he brushed aside more thoughts of his friend's unusual probing.

Breaking the silence during the long drive home, Eric impulsively opened his innermost thoughts to his companion. He told his buddy that until Olivia came along, he was ambivalent about love because he didn't want to be hurt again. He somehow believed his relationship with Jasmine had impacted him emotionally in the worst possible way.

Brinks casually asked, "Would you marry Olivia?"

Eric didn't hesitate to respond. "Sure I would. Everything I've experienced with her is good. All good.

There is no one like her."

As Allen negotiated congested traffic on the six-lane highway, he reacted to Eric's testimony, "Really, Man?"

"Absolutely. We have a connection that's emotional, spiritual, and I gotta' say, even physical."

"Whoa! Hold up. Nah, Bro. I don't wanna' hear any racy stuff." Allen laughingly stopped Eric from continuing.

"Don't worry, I didn't intend to give you any details, Man. I respect Olivia way too much to go there. But we do have something really special together."

When his companion tapped the accelerator and pushed ahead of a long line of cars, Eric quietly reflected on times spent with Olivia. He was convinced he loved her. It was not just the physical connection that confirmed his desires, it was much more... he realized his sentiments had gone miles beyond lust. With her, it was the epiphany of liberation from pent-up misgivings about love. So, for that reason, he knew his previously damaged heart was now in a good place – a place where it had never been.

Fifteen minutes and several miles later, a billboard promoting local restaurants popped up. Brinks was getting hungry and suggested a quick stop before pushing faster to be home by dusk.

When they got off the exit ramp, they decided to stop at a large mall; it was a rare site because malls were becoming national dinosaurs - with major department stores shuttering and the mega buildings turning into commercial ghost towns. Inside the moderately busy complex, the pair found a Chinese eatery. Eric, who was a fan of Asian food, was amused by a line of hungry customers that coiled the food court. He laughed to himself about how it was probably the best food at a reasonable price.

While ordering the lunch special, a fine jewelry boutique caught his eye. He planned to check it out.

"I'm gonna go across the way before we leave," Eric said pointing to the boutique.

"No problem," Allen replied and selected an entrée from options listed on the oversized menu board.

The two men ate quickly. Having a bite was now a lesser priority. Minutes later, he browsed the boutique window and went inside. Diamond bracelets, necklaces, rings, and studded earrings were there. Although buried in an array of choices, a locket caught him. The 14K-gold, one-inch pendant was a simple square except for the scroll design along its edges. A princess-cut diamond was in the center, and a tiny clasp opened to a perfectly smooth surface inside. It elegantly draped from a twenty-inch chain.

Eric asked the salesclerk about it and made the purchase for eight hundred and ninety-five dollars. Brinks curiously eyed him, confounded by the sudden buy, and wondered about his intentions.

Noticing that Brinks was puzzled, Eric asserted, "I want her to know I love her. I say it a lot, but my words are not always clear and it has plenty to do with my damned past; I just want her to understand what she means to me."

Brinks nodded agreement while listening to his friend who innocently uncovered his emotions. He bought the locket and had it gift-wrapped. The clerk recommended a red velvet jewelry box lined with white satin. She covered the box in shiny cerise paper to represent his heart and tied a white, glittery ribbon around it.

Leaving the store feeling proud of his decision, he thanked Allen for reassuring him.

Back on the road, Brinks asked once again if he was sure about the purchase. Eric turned sideways toward Allen and spoke.

"Allen, come on, Man. What are you really asking me?"

His friend said, "Well, you know, anytime you give a woman something like that, they kinda' think it's supposed to mean something else. Something more."

"Huh?" He was confused by Allen's chauvinistic commentary. "This necklace is just one way of expressing my love to Olivia."

Allen said, "But you give up a lot, Man. You know, saying goodbye to those old rules of hookups; it becomes a commitment thing. It's thought of as more than just kicking it on the weekend or just a casual hang out."

"Okay. And you and Shannon have more than a casual relationship, right?"

"We do, Eric. We do."

"So, I know you get where I'm coming from." With a peculiar look that foretold his feelings, Eric said again, "I was monogamous with Jas, remember? I'm not into dating around. I'm not interested in having a bunch of women. Not me, Allen."

Eric continued, "Olivia is an incredible woman. To be clear, I've learned that she is not defined by me or the material things I can give her."

His friend stayed mum, listening intently. Eric kept talking. "She is independent and knows exactly what she wants for herself. She knew what she wanted long before meeting me. I'm just happy to have her in my life. I'm even happier that I'm in hers."

"Sure, Man, I get it." Allen commented. "I understand everything you're saying, Bro."

"The bullshit that I went through with my wacky ass past transformed me. When things went south with Jasmine, that was it for me. But you know, I have since realized that I still have this thing about romantic love, even if it may be crazy to some people. That will never change about me, Allen. Today, I'm wiser and a helluva' lot more mature due to the previous shit in my love life. That's all," attested Eric.

Brinks continued to nod as he focused on the traffic. "It sounds like love to me, Eric. I was just checking."

He turned to Brinks, looking squarely at him with his brows pinched together, "That is exactly what it is. I've never been more certain of what I feel for her than right now."

"Cool, Man," said Brinks, cautiously moving along the roadway with other speeding cars. For the remaining miles, they talked about their ongoing design contracts, upcoming Thanksgiving Day plans, and NFL rankings.

It was the first day of December, at 1:30 A. M.

"Hello?"

"What are you wearing?"

Olivia recognized her lover's voice coming through the phone. "What are you up to at this hour?" She devilishly questioned him.

"What do you have on that beautiful body of yours right now?" He asked again.

"Just the lovely gold locket you bought for me on your way from Sacramento."

"And what else," he asked of her.

"Only the locket. Want me to prove it to you?"

"Yep. I do. I don't know if I can trust a physicist." She grinned at his remark and softly said, "Proof is seeing it for yourself. Why don't you come over here and find out. Seeing is believing. Use my code at the gate."

"Can you handle me if I get to you in fifteen minutes?" He dared her playfully.

"You're on." A short time later, he would be tapping on the front door. The door was half-opened, his face lit by a full moon glistening off the onyx sky.

She naughtily asked, "What can I do for you, Mr. Blake?"

"I couldn't sleep. I need you next to me."

"Come on in. Let's find a way to help each other get some rest." Locking the door behind him, he inclined against it, gazing at her seductively naked body while admiring her lovely face and black curly strands spilling off her shoulders. It was intimately soul-stirring. He couldn't decide what affected him most of all. Yet falling in love with her was becoming his wildest obsession. In the best possible way, being with her was a constant longing and an insatiable desire. He'd once whispered in a heated moment, "Woman, You are so damned addictive." He was beginning to believe that his confession about his desires was true, especially then.

He reached out to playfully pull her into a kiss. Instead of surrendering, she turned and pushed her hips against him. He pressed his lips to her neck and delighted in the taste of her brown skin. Showing satisfaction at how his hands felt on her, she exhaled and leaned back into his embrace.

"Come with me," she invited.

He followed her to the second floor, clinging to the captivating image of a pecan-brown, desirable woman for whom he had fallen. Just as they were about to enter her bedroom, she stretched her arms to block the doorway, then turned and asked, "Since you asked about it when you called, how do you like what I'm wearing?"

Approvingly, he examined the diamond-studded locket. She smiled up at him with eyes of love and waited for his reply. He answered in a whisper, "I like it. The man who bought it for you has excellent taste and loves you very much."

"Yes, he does," she provocatively agreed, lifting her height for him to examine it closely. "Can't you see how beautiful it is and why I also love him as much, too?"

He smiled. Olivia leaned back while his tongue stroked the well of her neck. His mouth tenderly tugged the chain and wantonly kissed her naked shoulder. She gave no resistance to his loving touch. In the dimmed room, she led him to the bed where hesitation was abandoned for desires that needed fulfillment. And the unrestrained love she needed poured from him. Filled with wanting, he explored every inch of her, and the sensuality that came over him from holding her provoked his emotions even more. She reached up to caress his shoulders, but he took her arms and gently forced them back to the bed.

"Please, Baby," he whispered, "let me love you."

Responding to his asking, she pouted her lips and whispered, "I want you right now, Eric, please. I want you all over me."

He kissed her sweet, ruby lips, carefully admiring every secret freckle, mole, and other perfection of her beautiful skin, onto where he kissed her waiting breasts. Inhaling the lustful scent of her made him unleash his indulged pleasure. He moved lower to make sure that she knew he was there, while making gentle waves with his tongue as if signing his name in her most private places. The subtle coarseness of his mustache sensuously tickled her inner thighs, causing her to answer his every touch.

She repaid his tender caress and gently released her hold on the bed to cling to him tightly. During those raw, emotional minutes, they were bound by pure and complete unanimity. And by now, the gift of love to each other was uninhibited. Their sensual copulation, was a gentle and forceful back and forth, where their affections flowed, and where breathing words of love in physical union felt right. She was learning the ways of real love and the delectation of being pleased by him. And he was falling deeper in love with her.

After the affectionate lovemaking, he held her. For a time, they remained wrapped in each other and quietly talked of the pleasure they'd shared. With only skin between them, she said satisfyingly, "Why don't you stay with me the rest of the night because we need to get some rest."

He answered her as he admired the golden locket glistening between her breasts, "I will if you'll keep wearing this beautiful outfit you have on."

Chapter 11
Confidence

The sabbatical in England drew near, and Olivia switched gears to complete the last preparation details. She finalized the university travel protocols by the month's end and signed a lease for housing in the foreign, unfamiliar city of Birmingham. On Monday morning in the office, she started checking off the to-do list by calling the office manager for updates on the upcoming departure. As usual, Ms. Marshall was on it.

"Good Morning, Ms. Marshall. How long will it take before Dr. Coleman finalizes my leave papers?"

"She has em' now. I think she will sign off on em' today."

"Thanks. I want to deal with my travel plans as soon as possible."

"Sure, Dr. Reece. Dean Coleman has prepared the memo with the list of sabbatical candidates. Everyone will get the email."

"How many are on the list from our department?" Olivia asked and casually leafed through the reports and publications brought to her by the graduate assistant.

"Only two. At first, there were three candidates, but the number changed."

"How did it change?" Olivia asked, seemingly puzzled.

"Remember, Dr. Strong in Biology has asked to wait until next year and Dr. Bledsoe is out now."

Olivia then remembered that Dan Bledsoe rejected Dr. Coleman's offer to be emerita. He protested, but lost the complaint filed with the union. He resigned abruptly. Everyone believed his decision to leave UST was triggered by a history of mean-spirited behaviors over the years. In his anger toward UST, he joined a private consulting firm that bid for contracts with the government. For many, his departure was a relief.

Olivia reacted to Ms. Marshall's update, "Oh, yeah. That's right."

"Is there anything else, Dr. Reece, because Dr. Coleman has just walked in," the Office Manager insisted, rushing to get off the phone.

"I'm glad to know you've taken care of this. Thanks again, Ms. Marshall." She replied with a goodbye.

That same day, Olivia was ready to dismiss her Quantum Mechanics students when Cliff Pinyin asked for clarification regarding a two-hour lab. He pointed to a page indicating students' requirements in the lengthy syllabus.

Cliff was among the brightest and most promising students in the rigorously demanding class. He was incredibly sharp in physics principles, and she believed he understood the fundamentals better than most of his peers. She'd often reminded him that his unique talent, passion, and sound diligence would pay off after college.

Cliff's curious and hardworking nature caused him to ask many questions in class, so his inquiry was no surprise. And although she encouraged every student to participate actively, Cliff's restless learning style was always refreshing.

The hands-on quantum class made it necessary for

some sessions to convene at remote locations, including the offsite lab. The next class, per the syllabus, required students to meet in Minion Hall initially and then take a shuttle to a remote lab nearly eight miles away. Some students, obviously prompted by Cliff's complaint, grumbled about having to leave campus. Other students chimed into the complaint, further attempting to strengthen their case.

The professor reminded them that the schedule of classes and lab sessions had been posted on the campus website long before the semester started, and she would not alter it for convenience. Their complaint developed into an unusually tense exchange with Dr. Reece, who was generally amenable to most student concerns.

Since she was unwilling to compromise, some disgruntled students walked out, disappointingly shaking their heads. One female student flung her hands upward, flipped her long brown hair, and quickly left the room. Across from her, an African American male remained seated and cautiously watched others bunch into several small groups to vent. He finally got up and left, choosing not to interact with anyone.

Cliff, the lead protester by default, stepped forward to argue on behalf of the group that remained with him and formed what appeared to be a motley united front.

"Dr. Reece, our next lab is a real problem for everyone. It takes us to another place away from Minion Hall."

Right off, Olivia was patiently dismissive. Unshaken by Cliff's dramatic plea, she ignored his criticisms and answered. "I'm sorry that the location of the upcoming lab is causing such worry for you, but this course was set in stone long before you arrived at UST this semester. Furthermore, this semester is almost over, Cliff, and all previous labs have been held there this term. Have you forgotten?"

"I know, Dr. Reece, but…"

"Let's see. How would you like it if I decided it is inconvenient for me to teach at 8:00 A.M.?" She paused, allowing him to digest every word. His blank face offered no response.

She continued, "You know, that could mean students who need this course might end up waiting another year before it is offered again. They would probably not graduate on time. Are you following me?"

"But hear me out, Dr. Reece…" He tried convincing her.

"Well, Mr. Pinyin, I don't have the privilege of setting up the schedules, and I would not want you to delay your graduation due to my failure to be a responsible professor." She asserted, then paused again, "And heaven forbid I found the 8:00 A.M. course too inconvenient for me."

"Okay, Dr. Reece, I think I know what you're driving at."

"I want you to get the picture, Mr. Pinyin. In physics, the most salient virtues are dedication and commitment. If you don't commit to everything the physics program offers, you will likely become a mediocre scientist. As dedicated researchers, we do what we must and persevere or stick it out, even when we don't want to. Do you see where I am going with my point? I hope you get it."

"Yes, I do."

"Good." she said, looking at the bewildered group, "I get it, too. I've been where you are now and know how difficult it is to balance your complicated lives as students. But remember that I have your interests in mind. I will work with you, but my high expectations of you won't falter."

The professor looked sternly at the group and restated her comments making sure the frustrated huddle heard every word, "I look forward to seeing all of you in the lab next week."

Though dissatisfied, the remaining students left the lecture hall with the failed leader, Cliff Pinyin, in tow.

Megan, the graduate assistant, whose reaction was less than discreet, flipped her heavily eye-lashed blue eyes and mumbled, "It's ridiculous, isn't it?"

Olivia deliberately ignored Megan's innuendo and feeble attempt to discuss what happened.

"Now Megan, our next meeting is set for Wednesday at 3:00 P.M., in my office. Bring your prospectus so we can discuss your recent changes. Several data points need a thorough review."

"Yes, Ma'am."

"I'm especially concerned about the stats I reviewed in your prospectus the other day. This needs to be addressed."

"Yes, Dr. Reece."

"It is important for you to stay on track for writing and defending your dissertation within two years. You do want to finish this program soon, don't you?" The professor was stern yet kind.

"Oh yes, Dr. Reece, I do."

"Good. Make sure to email me your notes from today's class before the day's end. I want to review what was covered and to take a look at the feedback we got from our students."

"I'll email it to you by five o'clock." Olivia heard the grad assistant repeating the promise as she exited the lecture   hall.

Professor   Reece   answered   without looking up at her. "I'll see you Wednesday, Megan."

At UST, it was an acceptable practice for students to raise concerns with professors on reasonably valid issues. Although Cliff's questions were reasonable, there was no valid reason to adjust the schedule.

Chapter 12
Unconditional

By afternoon, the test of patience with her students broiled in her. She fumed as she contemplated the need for a stiff drink as a way to wash thoughts of the disgruntled students from her. It was the same remark about drinking that her father would make when he'd had a tough day at work. But she rarely drank alcohol, except for one glass or two of wine with friends and an occasional shot of bourbon with Eric.

What she would not admit to Eric or her best friend, Lora, was that Lillie Reece had just about conditioned her to dislike drinking altogether. Sadly, for many years, her mother found solace in brown and colorless inebriating liquids, and she did this in the secrecy of her home. Olivia believed Lillie drank so much to escape a hurtful past, an episode that tinted an otherwise perfect life for Lillie.

Lillie's drinking had become an expected ritual. At the end of each day, she consumed martinis to wind down. This was her way of unbinding anguish and acquitting locked-up disappointment in her husband.

The marital damage tormenting her was because of Edward's infidelity that happened two decades before. The brief but sordid affair had been with an employee at T. S. Brogan. He was the woman's supervisor and blamed their illicit behavior on having to be in a close working environment.

When Edward's shameful dealings were made public, the woman caved to office embarrassment and left the company for a management job in Dallas. He was remorseful about cheating on his wife and wanted to put the wrongdoings of the affair behind. He'd tried for Lillie's forgiveness more times than could be counted, and she repeatedly promised to excuse the ugly incident of betrayal. But she didn't forget, and it was even harder for her to forgive.

It saddened Olivia that her mother would occasionally bring up Edward's transgressions during moments of anger. In those volatile times, nothing consoled Lillie and Olivia saw no end to her mother's sporadic contentions with Edward.

Desiring to make things better between them, Edward once tried to mend the widening crack that damaged their marriage by appealing to her to join him in counseling sessions. After one half-hearted attempt at discussing their problems with a counselor, they gave up. Even with the broken trust he'd caused, Edward Reece was determined to be faithful from then on. But he'd also sadly realized that the needless hurt imposed on Lillie was probably irrevocable. Still, in the midst of this, the unpleasant scars of Lillie's drinking stayed tucked behind the walls of family secrecy.

Her parent's occasionally stormy marriage started years before Olivia went off to college, and there was no apparent solution to their troubles in those days. She was much too young to understand what was happening between two wounded hearts. How could she possibly help her mother get past the hurt when her father, too, ignored his wife's emotional state? It was as if he and Lillie hoped the deed of infidelity would simply vanish on its own.

Often, in the middle of the night, she heard the fights and accusations between her parents. The verbal weapons, thrown in both directions, damaged Edward and Lillie's union. And over time, the couple's sporadic arguments were too painful for Olivia to endure. Because of that, she spent hours volunteering at a physics lab on the Santa Cruz Campus. There, she dug into her obsession with science. She voraciously read science journals and old science textbooks daily. She rarely engaged in a social life, such as spending time on social media, which was the typical amusement for young people her age.

Dr. Richard Chin recognized Olivia's potential in physics and willingly mentored her. Time away from her parent's hotbed of turbulence sharpened her knowledge and helped her snag an academic scholarship in the East. In an indeliberate way, each moment of the family chaos was a blessing for her future.

Many years of watching her mother suffer from alcoholism had been painful. Now, as a professor, it caused her to have empathy when people spoke harshly about co-workers they suspected of living with drinking problems, such as Dan Bledsoe. Because of Lillie, alcoholism affected Olivia personally; thence, she guarded her words about people with such problems and stayed away from senseless, unproven gossip.

On the other hand, she liked meeting friends after work, and a restaurant or bar was always the place to commiserate. So, after the incident with Cliff and the other students that afternoon, she wanted to let her hair down to blow off some steam. She phoned Lora and said. "Hey, Girlfriend, what's up with you now?"

Lora's answer was noisy. She was finishing off the last bites of a Caesar salad, which she was apparently enjoying. The loud crunching sound of croutons crackled as Olivia listened, so she moved the phone inches away from her ear.

"I'm having a late lunch. I had to ride east to two counties, which took up the first half of my day."

Olivia's friend took a gulp of liquid, swallowed loudly, and bit into more salad. Then, the noisy crunching started again.

"Well, you need a drink after a morning drive like that, don't you? Can you meet me at Garcia's in about an hour? My students wanted to change the lab schedule, which didn't sit right with me. The nerve of them!"

"That ticked you off, huh?" Olivia then remembered the mean-spirited behavior of Dr. Brian Hooperman in her freshman year. He had challenged her credibility, which markedly affected how she valued her own students. During the incident with Dr. Hooperman, she initially felt defenseless. However, for Cliff and his fellow students, it was crucial to maintain mutual respect between student and professor. She intended not to relinquish her authority as the instructor but was sensibly empathetic, too. She refused to be like Dr. Hooperman.

"Why don't you come over to Garcia's? I need someone to bounce my frustration off, and you're it."

Olivia invited Lora, especially now hoping to stop the sound of her attacking the crisp lettuce and croutons.

"Humm, that sounds good, but no thanks. Gotta' pass

on the offer. I want to finish this report before the Christmas Holiday starts." Lora interjected. Plus I wanna' get down at your folks party without thinking about work 'til after the new year." The crunching stopped for a minute as Lora waited for Olivia's reply to her apology.

"Alright, Lora. I was gonna' buy you a drink. And I'm talking about the top-shelf brand that I know you like and is only found at Garcia's."

"Can we record that promise?" Lora teased.

Though Olivia was making a soul-hearted attempt to entice her friend, she knew there would have to be a raincheck, realizing that her plan to hang out would not be happening.

"Okay, Lora." Olivia laughingly ended the plea with a reminder about the holiday party. Lora confirmed with a noisy bite of salad.

"I won't accept any excuses when we meet at my parent's house on December 16th. I promise you two drinks when you get there."

"Not to worry, Girlfriend. I will be ready to have a good time. That party is the best thing for me during the holidays."

"For sure," Olivia responded.

Chapter 13
Soiree

As usual, Lillie Reece was persistent when she asked, "Eric is coming to the party, isn't he?" She aimed to learn more about her daughter's friend but was also trying hard not to invade Olivia's privacy.

"Mom! Why are you asking me this?" Olivia questioned her, wanting to figure out where her mother's subtle interrogation was going. She knew Lillie would not give up on pursuing details about Eric. Lillie was ceaseless when it came to such things.

"I know that Lora and her friend Keith and your other friends will come. They always do, Honey, but I'm just making sure he is, too." Lillie echoed anxiously on the phone.

"Mom, if he comes, he comes. I don't dictate what Eric does. It's not like we are engaged to be married or any such foolish thing. For Heaven's sake, we are still just spending time together. We're okay with the way things are. You should be, too."

"Of course I am, Sweetie. I'm just trying to finalize the headcount so the caterer won't overcharge me." Olivia didn't intend to buy into her mother's flimsy rationale. It was apparent that Lillie's explanation was filled with holes since a budget for the party had been decided upon months earlier.

Olivia jokingly responded to her mother's slim argument. "As much of a stickler for counting pennies as Dad is, I doubt there will be any overcharging for this party. He has that part down pat, don't you think, Mom?"

"You're probably right. When I told your father I was about to start planning for the party this year, he asked for a budget. Can you imagine that? He does this every time. My goodness, we have been together for almost forty years. You would think he'd be used to my spending habits by now."

"I know, Mom." It took a long time for her to answer Lillie. She rolled her eyes, knowing her mother couldn't see the halfhearted expression through the phone. Lillie further agonized.

"God love him; he's hilarious sometimes. Even if he doesn't care about how much we spend on it, he always wants to be sure we've got a good deal on everything. Lord have mercy!"

"Right." Her daughter cradled the phone in the crook of her neck as she put dishes away and munched on walnuts and almonds. Her mother was chatting on and on.

"You do know your aunt and uncle are coming from Boston, don't you? Grace and I were on the phone talking about the party for nearly an hour yesterday. They booked their tickets months ago with plans to fly here a day early."

"I'm glad they're coming. How is Uncle Brad doing after his surgery?" Olivia responded.

"Grace says he is doing fine as long as he follows the doctor's orders," she said, "Brad is a lot like his big brother; he's stubborn just enough to make you want to do something crazy to em' – men are like that, you know."

"Like what?"

"Never wanting to appear vulnerable, especially with health and their hearts, hiding emotions and so forth."

"You're so intuitive, Mom. That's why I love you." Lillie delighted in Olivia's affirmation of love toward her and let go of a quiet laugh about her daughter's confessions regarding the nuances of life and love.

"As much as I love you and your dad, too."

"Mom, when you've put this party together every two years, it has been a big success. Everyone raves about it until the next one."

"Yes, I guess that's true. Thanks for saying that. This year is important for us because you're going to England a few weeks later."

"I'm excited about the sabbatical."

"I know your friend Eric will miss you, won't he?"

"Look, Mom," she appeared irritated and annoyed.

"Why are you so interested in what is happening between us?"

Lillie answered, "I just want you to be happy. That's all."

"And the point you're making, Lillie Reece?" Olivia reacted curtly to her mother's seemingly words of concern. Likewise, Lillie was rattled by Olivia's brusque comeback and wasn't aware of the recent argument her daughter had with Eric.

"Honey, I know you like him and I've realized he is a nice man. I'm just hoping we will get to know him better, Baby."

"If things continue, I'm sure you will."

"Really? Are you two getting serious?"

"Momma!"

"Okay, Olivia. I'm sorry. You're right. We should be talking about the party."

"Mom, I do have to go now. Love you."

"Bye, Baby. I think I will have a drink to kickstart my

planning. I have plenty of things to get done. I'll be calling on you for help." The young woman considered the disappointing fact that her mother was about to have a drink so early in the afternoon.

Mrs. Reece was the classic example of ageless beauty. She needed very little make-up and her youthful genes kept her age a mystery to anyone who didn't know her well. And though her drinking was frequent, she maintained an astonishingly healthy appearance.

She had a vibrant personality and was known to keep busy. Whether volunteering at the neighborhood school or helping with a charitable event at her church, you could always rely on Lillie to have her hands in it.

Her friends and associates praised the Holiday party. Altogether, she invited at least fifty guests. The people Olivia knew from UST, Edward and Lillie's former coworkers, and a few neighbors always showed up. She had also arranged for a block of rooms with a local hotel if any guests needed to stay overnight. So when extra people came along, Lillie never turned anyone away.

Minding the details, she wanted everything to be perfect for the biennial party. Her reputation of nineteen years living in Santa Cruz would depend on it. And she was not about to give in to compromising on any details of the event. Lillie had chosen the best caterer in Santa Cruz, who was expensive but highly sought after, and decided on a substantial budget for good liquor and wines. Plus, a DJ would be spinning music for anyone who looked forward to dancing, like Brad, her brother-in-law from back East.

The 16th of December arrived. By then, Eric and Olivia had been together with her parents a few times before, but this gathering would be significant. And because of that, he didn't want to disappoint her relatives or close friends by falling short of their expectations. He straightened the collar on his blue shirt and smoothed the double pleats in gray slacks cinched with an Italian leather belt. Perfectly shined cordovan wingtips finished off his look. Just before stepping out the door, he went back for his leather flight jacket in anticipation of a chilly December evening.

As he drove to Santa Cruz, his contemplations remained on Olivia and how his ideas on love had changed after meeting her. Thoughts of how far their love had come resonated in him. He was viewing their relationship in a different light. When he was younger, he believed that letting a woman know how much you cared too soon was a male weakness. But at this point, that didn't matter. He was finished with those old-fashioned ways. Such thinking had been a part of his immature, bravado past. Now, he was comfortable with what existed between him and Olivia. He wasn't afraid to reveal the depth of his affection for her.

Although he didn't want to predict too far into the future, he was enjoying what they had together. After their quarrel, she said the sabbatical would help cement their bond in a meaningful relationship.

"Maybe a little time apart," she'd offered, trying to assuage his fears of any possibility of a breakup. Needless to say, for him it was a little disconcerting that the active love affair was about to be put on hold for nearly a year. He could not explain it. Perhaps experiencing trustworthy love would be tested for the first time while she was away.

Exit 16B to Santa Cruz city limits was just ahead, according to the GPS. The familiar voice coming from the dashboard guided him.

"In 2.3 miles take exit 16B. Continue in the far-right lane. Traffic is congested ahead. Expect a six-minute delay before reaching the exit."

"Thanks," Eric said, unconsciously responding to the female navigator. His mind was on what it would be like amongst Olivia's family and friends once there.

The long driveway leading to her parent's ranch-style home was overflowing. As he backed his car into one of the last tight spaces, he could see a mixed crowd of Baby Boomers, Generations X and Y, and Millennials. After pausing and fighting butterflies, he walked in with the others. Guests were noisily socializing throughout the house and the backyard. The evening mood was festive.

There was endless food in every conceivable space. Top-shelf liquor poured generously and the number of people mingling at the different entertainment stations grew as friends swapped holiday greetings and hugs.

Out in the backyard, along a stretch of the tall privacy fence, large firepots glowed in contrast with the chilly winter afternoon. The leather jacket he'd brought along would likely come in handy later on. Eric greeted Olivia's parents with a gift of the best blanc de noir champagne that he could find. The couple was flattered. Lillie reciprocated his kindness with a kiss on the cheek and a hug and then led him to meet her friends.

"I want you to meet Eric Blake, Olivia's friend," she announced, glancing at the engineer with an effortlessly sly smile. She introduced him to a woman in her sixties sipping a frozen lime margarita. The woman swayed on two-inch-high heels as she tightly gripped the stem of a glass shaped like a cactus. She took sips of the drink and smiled back at him.

"Hi, Eric, I'm Susan Stark. I used to work with Lillie years ago."

Susan had a frumpy mass of frizzy platinum blonde hair that had apparently been permed way too many times. Salt granules from the margarita flecked the contours of lips slathered with bright orange lipstick. Around the woman's neck were layers of chunky turquoise and silver jewelry that weighed heavily on her thin frame. The jewelry appeared to test her frailty as she slowly rocked back and forth while looking up at Eric.

"This is my husband, Craig," she added, turning to the older man beside her. Susan's stout companion smiled, said nothing, and placidly gazed at the people dancing a short distance from where they were standing. Tapping his feet to the music, Craig looked more like a beer-drinking guy, and the half-filled glass of lime margarita looked out of place in his thickset hand.

"Nice meeting you," Eric politely said to the couple.

"Olivia is somewhere around here. She's been waiting for you, Eric," Lillie said, indicating her daughter's readiness to see him. "I think she's a little worried about you."

"Yes, Ma'am," he responded.

"Oh, there she is," said Lillie, pointing to where guests were gathered across the backyard. By now, the crowd was getting bigger and livelier with Olivia among them.

He was glad Lillie had given him a way to part from her friends since he didn't know how to strike up a conversation with them. Turning and walking away, his social instincts kicked in as he greeted and carried on small talk with other guests nearby.

It was an interesting mix of personalities. At one of the food stations, Kip Thibodeaux was talking animatedly to onlookers about how to make New Orleans gumbo. Party guests always raved about it, so it had become one of the hottest items topping the menu. When Kip recognized Eric from the campus fundraising reception, he waved a friendly hello. And as if on cue, he went right back to giving a culinary chat. One could see that Kip was in his element, just as he would have been in the physics lab. Eric decided to listen as the professor entertained the group.

"I use a combination of the best and freshest ingredients. That's the secret." Kip's Cajun dialect flavored his explanation of cooking the thick creamy roux and adding, at specified times, andouille sausage, jumbo lumps of crab meat, and finally, the biggest shrimp of all.

"This process can take up an entire day. I used to watch my dad make it for years," explained Kip. It was easy to tell that Kip enjoyed engaging the group that waited to taste his masterpiece. The question of spiciness was brought up by someone among seven or eight party-goers listening in.

"Oh, that depends on how hot you can take it," he responded. "For Mrs. Reece's party, I try to keep the heat low so you don't curse me the next day." The group roared laughingly.

Across from Kip's attentive audience, Edward and three friends from T.S. Brogan Technologies sipped beers as they reminisced about days gone by. One of the men said something that threw them into gut wrenching laughter. Other men standing nearby were drawn to the group and joined the conversation. Their salt and pepper hair was evidence of an older and mature generation that represented years of wisdom. Eric warmly admired them and the successes they'd probably accumulated during many years of dedicated work. A trace of envy was felt as he watched them.

At another place in the backyard, younger guests were dancing alone or as couples to the DJ's jazzy hip-hop remix. Eric was tickled by an older pair who jumped onto the makeshift dance stage and pleaded with onlookers to join them in a line dance. Several others stepped onto the twelve-foot-wide platform and slid right into the sway of about ten people stepping and clapping their hands on every turn. They were doing the ever-popular electric slide. Soon, the group moved with such precision that age and generational differences could no longer be distinguished. It was a few days before Christmas, and everyone was joining the festivities of the holiday season. Eric curled his back against a corner of the porch where others sat socializing and watching the dance floor moves. He couldn't hear Lillie calling out to him until the third attempt.

"Eric, I want you to meet someone." She called again. He turned and started in Lillie's direction. When there, he apologized for not hearing her and greeted the others.

"I'm Sorry, Mrs. Reece. I couldn't hear you."

"That's no problem, Eric." She smiled and overlooked his apology. "I want you to meet Edward's brother and his wife from Boston, Brad and Grace Reece, and Doris, whom I think you've already met. This is Eric Blake, Olivia's friend." Doris casually flashed a friendly wave.

"How are you doing? I'm Brad." The man, slightly younger than Edward, smiled and firmly shook Eric's hand as he introduced himself. "This is my wife, Grace. They say you're from back East?"

Eric was poised, ready to answer. "Yes, Sir."

"Oh yeah? How long?"

"Coming up on several years; close to ten."

"How'd you end up here?"

"I earned my degree at State U with a degree in aeronautical engineering and started my career in aircraft design. I enjoy my work and like this part of the country."

"Oh yeah?" Brad asked.

"But my parents are back East - in Charlotte, North Carolina. I'm on my way there for the holiday. I go back home just about every year during this time." Eric wanted to offer a thorough response before Brad shot another question.

Although some years separated them, the younger Brad, shared good looks and mannerisms with Edward. Brad was friendly, as was his wife, and they made Eric feel at ease. He liked them instantly.

"Well, Eric, we are in Boston. I'm a state government worker ready as hell to retire, and I'm almost there. Next time you come cross-country give us a shout. Love to see you, Man. Our two sons would love to meet you, too"

"Thanks, I'll do that, Sir. It is nice meeting you and Mrs. Reece. And it's nice to see you again, too, Ms. Doris." He then turned to Olivia's mother.

"Excuse me, Mrs. Reece. I'm gonna' make my way over to see Olivia." He said goodbye. Even though he enjoyed being with everyone there, he was excited about his plans to leave the party for some private time with Olivia. After leaving the Reeces, who were now entertaining others, he caught a glimpse of Olivia with guests on the far side of the yard. She was in a lively conversation with an older man and woman. The beige turtleneck sweater against her beautiful skin caused uninhibited fondness for her. He couldn't help but treasure every bit of what he saw; she was entrancing and watching her from afar conquered his heart. He could hardly wait. He had a surprise to share, so he moved in her direction.

Stopping briefly to speak with two twenty-something men in his path, and talking with others, he was finally beside her. She was eager to introduce Dr. Chin and his wife.

"I've heard a lot of good talk about you, Eric," Dr. Chin spoke as he shook the younger man's hand with a warm greeting.

"Yes," Eric responded, smiling sincerely. "And I have heard much about you, too, Sir."

The older professor humbly blushed and thumbed a friendly gesture toward Olivia, "Your friend here is a superb scientist. She tells everyone that I influenced her. Likewise, I've learned a lot from her, too."

"Yes, Dr. Chin. I can say the same. I know a lot more about physics since meeting her."

The casual talk between the two couples continued for a short time afterward. All the while, Eric was eager to be alone with Olivia. He privately whispered, "Wanna' ride with me?"

"Yeah. That sounds great." She'd given in to the joy of finally being with him. "Whatcha' got in mind?"

"You'll see. I've got something special for you. I think you'll like it."

"Okay. I won't tell Mom and Dad we're leaving. Even better than that, I'll text Lora after we're outta' here. She can tell Mom. With all these people here, she won't miss us."

"Good idea. I'm gonna' leave that thorny part to you." He set his empty wine glass on a table near the bar, gently squeezed her hand, and began directing her to the door. "Let's go," he urged, getting more enthused about being alone with her. They could hear everyone cheering the line dancers before closing the front door. And by now, Brad and Grace Reece had joined the crowd on the dance floor. Olivia smiled broadly with anticipation of an adventure. She, too, was ready to leave the party to be alone with him, and the couple sneaked away.

Before long, they were driving down a winding back road known as state road 329 toward the small nearby town of Kenmore. Daylight was slowly fading. After a fifteen minute drive, they arrived at the entrance of an airfield where single-engine planes were cloistered in a giant hangar. The large metal and concrete building stood alone in the middle of a grassy, nearly barren field. All else seen was a tar-black, mile-long strip of asphalt that stretched over a mile. Oddly, she knew very little about the small, sparsely populated town, even though it was just a short drive from where her parents lived.

"Where are you taking me," Olivia asked excitedly. She squeezed Eric's hand that rested on her thigh. "Gotta' show you somethin'."

The hangar was enormous. Stored inside were five planes, all of them privately owned, and built for six to eight passengers. A man wearing a green shirt with the name Albert inscribed on the pocket. His bushy blonde hair didn't match the thick, brown mustache that partially obscured his upper lip. Albert had several airplane tattoos on large biceps forcibly squeezed into tight shirtsleeves.

At first, he showed no awareness of the couple when they walked in while talking away on a phone call. Boisterous laughter followed words spoken to the person on the other end of the line. He, at last, got around to a chuckling goodbye.

"What can I help you with," he asked as he peered at the couple with suspicious eyes.

"I'm Eric Blake. We have a reservation for a Piper Turbo."

The man's attitude suddenly turned cordial. "Oh, yes, Sir. We have that for you in hangar three. We can taxi it out to the runway for you. First, I need to verify your Aviation Administration certification credentials, a valid photo ID, and a credit card to collect the charges.

That'll be three-hundred-twenty-five dollars."

"Thanks," said Eric.

"You will have access to the plane for an hour.

"That's fine," Eric confirmed.

Throughout the entire transaction, Olivia was dumbfounded. She finally found words to ask, "Are you seriously going to fly that plane?" She waved a hand in the direction of the third plane.

"Yes, and you're going to take a flight with me, right?" He pointed a finger toward himself. "We know how to fly planes, too," Eric teased.

He tilted his head and stared at her through devoted eyes. His doting smile pleaded with her to accept his invitation. Because she was so busy planning for England, she hadn't noticed the time he spent completing the flight training. He often talked about wanting to fulfill the requirements but conversations about that were infrequent. Intended to be a surprise for her, it had been a well-kept secret after the sobering argument that happened weeks ago. Once he finished the transaction with Albert, he found her waiting for him near the entrance. She was without words.

"I wanted to surprise you before you go to England. Are you ready to fly with me, Beautiful Lady?" She reached out to hug him, saying how proud she was.

"This is great. You didn't tell me!" Being the least bit embarrassed by any possible audience, he pulled her to him and took pleasure from her kiss, finding enjoyment in her. Willingly, she melted into his arms, satisfied to feel his embrace. Then the cell phone in her pocket vibrated as he released her. She glanced at the caller ID and announced, "It's Mom."

She answered. "Hello, Mom. How's the party?"

"It is going well, but I miss you two." Her mom was lightheartedly blunt. "I wanted to make sure you and Eric are alright and that he didn't have an emergency."

"We're at an airstrip in Kenmore, Mom. This gorgeous man I'm with is going to take me out on a surprise flight before I leave for England."

"You're going to do what! You're where!"

Olivia was nonchalant. "He's taking me up on a flight in just a minute before it gets too dark. I would've told you we were leaving, but you were busy with everyone there."

"I texted Lora to let you know if you asked."

"She told me you left a while ago. I didn't realize you were gone. After I found out, I thought something was wrong."

"Nothing's wrong, and I'm fine, Mom. I am in the best care. We will be back before the party is over. I promise. We just wanted some time alone."

"I understand. You and Eric have fun. Just tell him I said to be safe with my daughter," Lillie chuckled, sounding full of liquid spirits.

It was a perfect first-time flight with him as a pilot. In as much as Olivia didn't know what to expect, she was nervous, but his handling of the plane calmed her fears, and their time together in the air was all she imagined. They touched down on the runway after an hour. By now, night had fallen.

"Thank you, Eric. You've given me the best Christmas gift that I could ever get."

"You are welcome," he lovingly said. That night, she opened her heart to him in a letter.

My Dearest Eric,
For the first time in my life, I've decided that my constant apprehension of loving you cannot take control of me. Instead, I must appreciate and enjoy the promise that I get from your love. What I want most is the happiness that consumes me when I'm with you and reassures me when we are apart. I am blessed because I'm yours.

Olivia

PART TWO

Chapter 14
Solo

Now, in January, Lillie would bid her daughter farewell as she prepared to leave for England. The young professor's sabbatical journey had begun years before when her father met physicist Richard Chin. During a chance meeting at Santa Cruz University, Edward told the distinguished professor about his daughter's keen appetite for science and asked for recommendations.

The coincidental meeting at Santa Cruz University began a lasting friendship. However, Lillie was concerned about how she and Edward's episodically turbulent relationship impacted her daughter's life.

Oddly, though, Lillie never gained the courage to talk about the couple's rocky marriage to anyone, especially Olivia. And the way Olivia was able to avoid her parent's tumult during her youth was working with Dr. Chin.

Now that Olivia was about to leave the country, Lillie promised herself to have the dreaded conversation when her daughter returned. She loved Olivia unconditionally and believed she was owed an honest discussion about the pain Edward had caused. Today, however, Lillie quietly gazed upward, with hands prayerfully clasped, and whispered, "Thank you."

Days later, Eric drove Olivia to LAX International on Imperial Highway then to the departure gates on World Way.

At the carrier departure gate, Eric didn't want to let Olivia go. He held her then gently pushed her away at arm's length so his eyes could drink her loveliness. He embraced her again and hugged her tightly, longing for her to stay.

"I want you to be careful, Babe."

"You know I will be," she answered. She didn't want to shed tears. She disliked the way her crying eyes always looked, puffy and bloodshot red after tearful moments like this.

"I'm serious, Babe. I want you back here with me in exactly eight months. No excuses. I'm already missing you."

"I'll call you as soon as I get there." She reached out to gently touch the curl of his lips, brought on by his attempted smile.

"Promise?"

"Of course, I will," was said as she motioned a pinky-finger promise back at him. He watched her walk toward the gate with the tan satchel hanging from her shoulder. Her most treasured possessions were in it, including two pictures of him that would be on her nightstand in Birmingham until she returned home. She glanced back one more time, knowing months would go by before seeing him. Hours later, she was in Europe.

Welcome to London. On arrival, the airport was teeming with travelers. Although she had flown to a few other Western European hubs in the past, this was her third trip to Heathrow. Prior stops in the United Kingdom, however, had always been brief and served as a connection to other destinations. From Olivia's viewpoint, London's airport had to be one of the busiest in the world.

She looked for gate signage as thousands rushed to many terminals that spiraled in every direction. The facility was easily navigated, even for the most inexperienced globetrotters. Thankfully, though, less than an hour separated her and the journey's end. Although she would be returning to London for the physics conference, Olivia was eager to leave the crowded facility. She soon boarded flight 330, the connecting flight to Birmingham, England.

Once in Birmingham, Olivia found baggage claim in typical airport confusion. Travelers edged past one another as they pushed closer to the luggage carousel, hoping to collect their recognizable luggage quickly. It was a funny sight, and Olivia discreetly laughed as she waited her turn. Her parents gifted her with twin pieces of designer luggage at Christmas. Though she fretted the pricy gift, she appreciated it because her old luggage might not have reached Europe before falling apart. Besides, her mother insisted that she travel in style with signature luggage.

Olivia thought fondly of her parents as she surveyed the uneven heaps of black, brown, and occasionally bright red bags cranking around the metal circular that made a continuous grinding sound. Her heart warmed as images of her parents came to mind.

"I gotta' call my folks as soon as I get a taxi," she reminded herself. "I hope international signals won't be a problem for me to call them."

She spotted one of her designer bags on the endlessly turning carousel and prepared to grab it. Gripping the handle quickly, she snatched it off the top of an equally large piece of black luggage and struggled to hoist it. A man nearby came to her rescue, lifted it, and placed it beside her. She immediately took the matching piece from the loudly cranking machine behind the first one. Then, turning to thank the tall man for his help, she discovered he was, by this time, walking among the horde of people moving in the direction of rental car pickup.

Olivia piled her leather satchel on one of two suitcases and pulled them to ground transportation. When there, she spotted a drove of black and white taxi cabs and waved for a ride. Like everyone else, she was caught up in the mass of weary travelers, glad to leave the crowded, overflowing airport behind.

A driver in taxi number twenty-seven met her gaze, moved forward, and jumped out of the car to offer his services. While he stacked her bags into the cab's trunk, she detected what might have been the melody of an African accent. He welcomed her to Birmingham and asked where she needed to go.

"Please take me to Harrington Avenue in Castle Vale. Oh, by the way, what will you charge me, please?"

Jovially fanning a black device resembling a portable GPS, the driver explained how rates were determined and gave her an estimated fare in Pounds, then U.S. Dollars. He said his cab service, one of the best, used a standard navigation tool to calculate the fare. Satisfied with his answer, she gave him the address and got into the car.

From the back seat of the taxi, she checked out her new surroundings as they left the airport property. All around her, departing cars inched along, and frustrated drivers honked to be allowed into lanes aiming for the exit. Her driver appeared irritated by the slow-moving cars and briefly spoke another language before sharing his location with the command center. To someone on the other end, he answered, "Thank you," along with several words in English, then refocused on the bumper-to-bumper traffic.

"Is it always like this?" She asked the driver, trying to be a friendly passenger.

"No. Not always, just twenty-four hours every single day!" He chuckled. It was his way of humoring the current customer. He continued, "It is like this, hum, how you say in America, ah, twenty-four-seven?"

Olivia politely laughed with him.

Following his offering of Birmingham insights, he didn't speak but repeatedly pounded the car's horn and dangerously pushed his way into the traffic flow. Scarily, he continued to dash in and out of a line of speeding cars, once swerving to avoid a potential accident with another car. After luckily surviving the close call, Olivia breathed relief.

No longer thinking of the driver's talent for avoiding mishaps, she texted her mom and dad with a promise to call them as soon as she could inspect the house and neighborhood. Thankfully, her mother responded and asked that she be thorough about safety. Days earlier, Lillie urged her to get information on law enforcement and emergency services nearest her. Her daughter would keep her promise.

Before she could dial Eric's number, her phone played his caller ID tune and displayed his picture on the phone's screen.

"I was getting worried. Are you okay?"

"Yes, Got here just fine. No worries. Hectic airports are everywhere. I wish I'd been able to get a direct flight to Birmingham instead of landing in London first." She was exhausted, but going to the extra airport had saved on airfare.

"What happened?"

"Nothing really. It was a bit of a problem finding my way around the terminals, even with the airport app on my phone, but it was not so bad. I'm in a taxi headed to Castle Vale now."

"You miss me?" he questioned naughtily.

"A little, I suppose."

He lowered his voice as if shielding his words from the taxi driver. "Woman, if I were there right now, I'd give you lovin' that you'd never forget."

"Well, my Dear, you'll have to wait months before that happens. Will eight months from now be too long for you to wait?"

"You will see me long before then." He spoke in a hoarse whisper.

"How is that possible?" She giggled aloud and looked up to discover the taxi driver listening and awkwardly smiling.

Eric teased, "Babe, I can't give away all of my secrets. Remember, planes fly to Europe every day."

She smiled as she listened to him thousands of miles away. As the reality of being away from home sank in, she started to miss him more. Was it a mistake to be gone from someone she loved as much for such a long time? For a second, she thought of asking the driver to take her back to the airport. But as the rush of her subtle desires left her. she was reminded of her commitment to researching abroad. She would call him from Castle Vale just as she had promised ger parents.

Wintertime in Birmingham. It was a city of old mixed with the new. Remnants of Industrial Revolution buildings shared the skyline with modern skyscrapers towering over a place that on first impressions appeared cold and gloomy. The January sun was struggling to show itself on an otherwise gray and cloudy sky; it was a canvas that teased humans with spasmodic marks of winter blue.

Pedestrians, stared at their cell phones and ambled past each other while hardly realizing where they were. Olivia viewed the obsession with cell phones as a realistic display of what people worldwide had become. In the new century, the absence of "human" interaction with one another was far more commonplace.

Humans were now depending on their electronic devices as essential appendages in every aspect of their lives. Such behavior, thought Olivia, made Birmingham, like many places across the globe, a treasure trove of research opportunities on device dependency, and how electronic devices related to the NASA sub-station project.

The fading art of interacting face-to-face would likely be interesting research. Since the dynamics of human interaction and technology mattered to her, Olivia's introspection caused her to wonder, "As a devoted physicist, did I have a hand in today's electronic madness, too?"

Morning traffic from the airport to Harrington Avenue gave her an idea of a daily commute in the moderately large city. It didn't appear to be all that bad. But the quietness inside the taxicab caused her to yearn for a time to focus solely on her work. Her main objective was to fully commit to the long-awaited opportunity in England. Her temporary home in Birmingham was a modest condo overlooking the River Tame. It was among the most exclusive properties in the Castle Vale subdivision. When she arrived at 7903 Harrington Avenue, a cheerful housekeeper handed over possession of the key. Her name was Jane. Jane's plump cheeks were bright red on milky-white skin, apparently kissed by the nippy winter.

Jane gave the new tenant a quick overview of the condo and answered general questions. Before leaving, she agreed to service Olivia's rental twice weekly, and the service rate would be settled the following morning. Jane's friendly goodbye was heartwarming, and it softened the professor's concerns about being in a new environment.

When Jane was gone, Olivia walked through the condo a second time. It was meticulous. Spotless. Dustless. There was a conservatory with a view of the back yard and the garden. A small library would also serve as an extra sitting room directly across from the main bedroom. She liked this windowless feature of the condo because it allowed her to work in a safe space during late hours.

Months earlier, in preparing for an extended stay abroad, she paid over eight thousand dollars in an advanced deposit to a real estate service called BritLands. The reputable company was praised by a UST professor who'd spent time in Birmingham during previous years. The condo was suitable housing for a single woman since safety was a major concern. She was now ready to settle in and get to work. But for then, she needed sleep.

Jetlag can make anyone feel weirdly screwed up. Anyone who has ever experienced it knows it can whack your entire rhythm of life for days. You will even feel like you're in a liminal, hazy state, all without sufficient sleep. And for Olivia, circadian dysrhythmia, aka jetlag, was no damn joke. It happened every time she traveled across a series of time zones. Covering thousands of miles to Europe had caused her to need more shuteye, and getting into bed early for several nights would likely help.

On the second night in the Harrington Avenue condo, the effects of jetlag were still present. It was dark at 9:00 P.M. in Birmingham, but the sun was still shining at 1:00 P.M. in California. Her discombobulated state of tiredness shrouded her clear thinking.

"Oh yeah, I'm in Europe!" she mumbled, still in a fog. She got out of bed briefly and again buried herself in the sheets for six more hours.

On the third morning, still recovering from traveling, she searched the kitchen shelves for coffee and something light to eat. The owner had left starter supplies, giving her time to become familiar with Castle Vale conveniences. Jane had happily provided Olivia with suggestions for the best places to shop for food and other essentials.

"Gotta' check these places out before losing myself in work," she determined, leafing through a stack of information left on the bedside table.

The following day, as sunrise ushered daylight onto the kitchen counter, Olivia made coffee and admired the floral landscape in her backyard. A ten-foot, ivy-covered cedar fence separated the manicured grounds of the semi-detached home. Every known winter flower, in every possible color, greeted her tired eyes. The smell of freshly brewed coffee persuaded her to explore the rest of the house under the glow of sunlight shining through pristine windows.

The small library, which would serve as her office, had a recessed mahogany bookshelf on the northside wall. Books of every kind filled the shelves. From a thorough examination, she found several publications, fragile with age and some dating back to the late 1800s. The owners of the property were obviously well-educated. The beautifully maintained place had more than a dozen remarkable features.

At 7:30 A.M. local time, her cell phone rang.

"Hello, This is Dr. Reece. How can I help you," she asked the unknown caller.

"Yes, Dr. Garfield here. I want to welcome you to Birmingham. We're very honored to have you join our research program this year."

"Yes, thank you, Dr. Garfield. I'm happy to be here." Olivia listened to the woman on the other end as she elaborated the vision of inviting her to the university.

The Birmingham professor thanked her American guest for accepting the temporary teaching assignment and said, "Having you here as a guest faculty will benefit Birmingham students greatly."

In the meantime, Olivia tried visualizing the woman's appearance. Her high-pitched voice suggested she might be petite, but that was only a guess. Even after many previous telephonic meetings, she had never met Garfield in person.

"Yes, Dr. Reece, of course, welcome. On behalf of my colleagues, I invite you to dine with us on Thursday evening at which time you will get a chance to meet the entire team. Does that sound agreeable to you?" The woman cheerfully inquired of Olivia.

"Oh yes, indeed," Olivia smiled as she responded, while enjoying the woman's British accent.

"Fine then," Garfield confirmed. "I shall meet you at your condo on Harrington Avenue, Thursday at 5:00 P.M. sharp."

"Thank you. I look forward to meeting all of you then, Dr. Garfield. Goodbye."

On the following wintry day in Birmingham, melancholy and loneliness consumed her. Meanwhile, back in San Honesto, a different kind of winter season had begun; she missed familiarity. Today, on her third day of watching an afternoon unfold, she called Eric. When his phone rang, a pouty smile with one of Olivia's playful, silly poses showed on his screen.

"Good morning. I know it is still early where you are, but I wanted to say hello," she said and listened to his waking and yawning sounds. His voice sounded scratchy as if his throat was cottony dry.

"Good morning to you, Beautiful. What time is it there?"

"It is already two o'clock here. How are you, Eric?"

He took a sip of water from the glass on the bedside table. "Doing fine. I'm finishing up a cockpit design proposal today."

"I hope it will be a good day for you." She responded, mimicking his yawn and stretching her arms upward.

"That's right." His voice trailed off as if being distracted by something in his bedroom.

"Are you getting settled in Birmingham?"

"Yes. My first meeting with the university team is tomorrow. It's a dinner meeting. One of the professors is giving me a lift from here, so I don't have to worry about getting around the city. Not just yet anyway."

"That's awesome, Olivia. Just stay safe."

She replied, "Thanks, Eric. I appreciate your care."

They talked for another fifteen minutes, with confessions of missing each other. Olivia reluctantly started to say goodbye because she had already been there for three days and needed to finish unpacking. However, the conversation didn't end. There was a trace of sadness in his voice, so she pushed for more. Something was tapping at her intuition, causing her to react to his reserved and somber mood.

"Is there something wrong, Eric?"

"Nah, not really. I talked to Mom yesterday. She questioned where I'm going with my life."

"What did your mom say?" Olivia listened to Eric's grievance as she touched the locket, which always touched her heart.

"Something about how she is looking forward to spoiling a few grandchildren before she dies. She went on and on about what her friends are telling her."

"Why do you think she feels that way?"

"Don't know exactly. I'm thirty-four, and my mom is trying to persuade me!" His scratchy voice rolled over the distance as his mother's words stormed through him.

"Eric, your mom loves you and she knows you would be an excellent father. Mrs. Blake understands you better than anyone else you've ever known. After all, she is your mother."

"Yeah, Olivia. I'm just glad I didn't have kids before I left my last situation," he answered, wanting to rid himself of the disturbing images of his past relationship. She intentionally ignored the harsh words deriding his former mate, desiring not to comment on a situation that happened long before her time with him. She changed the direction of her comments. "I think... No, Eric, I know you've made your mother extremely proud. And, Sweetheart, you will continue to make her happy. I'm sure she doesn't doubt your decisions. None of them."

"I don't know, Olivia." He reacted to her encouraging words. "Right now, Mom seems to have a different agenda for me."

"Hey, I think you are almost perfect." She was saying it jokingly to lessen his stress.

"Almost... humm." His response to what she said was unconvincing. Then, as if from nowhere, he asked, "Hey, Olivia, have you thought much about starting a family?" Caught off guard and unable to reply at once, she stopped short of an answer as her phone beeped an incoming call.

"Gotta' go. I'll call you later. Mom's ringing in now. Love you with all my heart." She switched lines to speak with Lillie.

"Hey, Mom!" She was overjoyed to hear from her mom who updated her on the shopping antics of Edward's sister, Doris. As everyone knew, Doris was the star of the family's most interesting events. Known for making the unexpected laughable, she always added colorful humor to everything she did. Lillie explained that Doris had persuaded them to travel nearly two hours north for a mega antique sale. Once there, after a very long journey, they found a scrappy older man with a warehouse filled with boxes of rubbish, as described by Lillie.

Edward was furious because he'd skipped a chance to spend time with retired buddies at a local sports bar.

"Needless to say," Lillie exclaimed, "Edward swore to never take us antique shopping again." Olivia knew Edward's threat to abandon the ladies was never intended. Not much had changed in Santa Cruz.

Long after hanging up with her mother, Olivia still could not dispense thoughts of what Eric said earlier. Throughout the day, his distressed mood troubled her, and she wanted him to know she understood his feelings. But Olivia hadn't found the right words to say when on the phone with him. So, in ole' school communication, she sent a handwritten letter to him on the finest, most beautiful linen stationery she could find.

Dear Eric,

I never imagined having a friend and lover who is the rare embodiment of strength, gentleness, kindness, and compassion. But in divine providence, God introduced me to you nearly a year ago. Since then, I've discovered countless qualities about you. Your aspirations and yearnings are in complete harmony with my values. I've realized that you have a phenomenal awareness of self — of your needs and desires, and through God's divine guidance, you confidently live those virtues daily. I admire you. I'm proud of you. I believe in you! My Love, I marvel at your consistency and admire your steadfastness. Each day, I understand you more, and I recognize why I should always protect God's gift of pure love that we share. I am genuinely thankful for what you've brought to my life.

Always yours, Olivia -

She mailed the letter the next day on the way to the university. The letter arrived days later, laced with her familiar fragrance.

Chapter 15
Difference

"Good morning. I'm Dr. Olivia Reece from the University of Scientific Technology in Southern California. Thank you for welcoming me. In the last week, I've had the chance to discover many fascinating facts about your historic university and this fascinating city. I hope to learn more about England during my stay, including the best places to get a good meal. There are way too many burger shops near UST, and dining here will be a refreshing change."

Subtle laughter about college culture came from the audience, whose curiosity about the American instructor was apparent. Seemingly, the professor's easygoing personality quickly ended worries about relating to college life.

"Until now, the only restaurant I've tried here in Birmingham is The Yellow Garden, where the food was superb." The students' agreement about the quality of the popular restaurant confirmed a mutual interest and was an easy opener for her.

Her first class began with an overview of the course she'd be teaching and a brief introduction to her research. Olivia paused for questions. There were none.

"I recommend you use our office contact information freely. My door is always open to discuss any challenges you may be having with physics. My role is to help you become capable of understanding the relationship of physics to quantum cryptography, quantum entanglement and cybersecurity. Together, we can get your understanding of this field at its best." She was ready to start class with a lecture on QFT (quantum field theory). "Okay, my good students, let's get going."

Over time, the British students came to appreciate her teaching style and gift of knowledge, particularly understanding the significance of particle physics in various aspects of encryption aimed at mitigating security breaches.

By the end of February and into early March, she had grown accustomed to the damp and cold conditions in the European city. She was enjoying her students and the meaningful, collaborative work with the faculty at Birmingham. However, as the days turned into months, the bleak, overcast environment made California increasingly desirable.

She was missing those nearest her heart. She missed her family. She yearned for everything familiar. The need was there, temporarily, to replace the loneliness of being in a foreign city without those she loved. To escape her blueish mood, she decided to head to Casey's Pub, not far from where she lived.

The pub, a famous Irish hangout only two and a half miles from Olivia's condo, was situated in an unusual place. Built on a concrete island that defied architectural common sense, the well-known hangout welcomed everyone. It was known as a friendly hub for local revelers. Many of the Castle Vale residents went there daily for happy hour.

This evening, especially, she needed a break from the depressing time, dampened by the seasonal Birmingham weather. If she went to Casey's Pub with plans for just one glass of wine, enough time would be left for additional writing when she returned home.

She activated the security system and walked onto the cobblestoned street where a blue taxicab, broadcasting the company's phone number in black and white paint, waited for her. The congenial cabbie, who knew the destination, drove toward the pub, deliberately avoiding the busiest city thoroughfares. The ride to Casey's would be short.

Glimmers of a fading afternoon bounced off the rugged street surfaces as the car rambled onward. En route, British life along the canals near a shopping district called Brindley Place revealed a peaceful scene that lifted her mood.

Birmingham had a fascinating old-world appeal. The city, which originated in the seventh century, stirred curiosity about what hid behind the tidy cottage doors along the taxi's path. This mystery made her want to explore the area even more before leaving the country.

Aware that she seemed genuinely interested in learning about his hometown, the affable driver took her on a scenic, winding drive through one of the historic neighborhoods. The excursion increased the fare, but mileage beyond her destiny had been well worth it. Ten minutes later, at the cab stand where she was dropped off, shoppers along the bustling storefronts were enjoying the occasional peeks of afternoon sun. She paid the fare, wrapped the scarf tighter to protect her neck and shoulders from the biting cold and stepped onto a sidewalk brimming with local shoppers and tourists.

A gregarious bouncer, who probably served no purpose other than to keep drunken partygoers in line, was guarding the pub's main entrance. He looked ruggedly imposing. His muscular and menacing build would have set fear in anyone - especially if their drunkenness ended up causing a loud ruckus. He pointed her toward a turnstile at the entrance. Surprised to see the apparatus, she pushed her weight against the three-pronged metal object and went inside. Irish folk music filled the room as she surveyed the packed area, which seemed relatively small for the number of people there. It was hard to tell, but there must have been well over a hundred patrons squeezed into the triangular-shaped building. Occupancy codes were not bound to local enforcement.

At the bar, familiar faces from her neighborhood kindly greeted her with nods and half-smiles. A group of familiar Castle Vale women who sat in a poorly lit corner waved and said hello as she edged by. Further inside, Olivia noticed a vacant barstool. She quickly seized it.

One man looked her way. He stood alone at the crowded counter, swallowing frothy beer from a hefty stein. Olivia recognized him as one of her neighbors. The flower bed in front of his house was a favorite landmark on her daily walk in the tidy community. His garden caused her to miss California even more. When she first arrived in Castle Vale, she asked him how he managed to have the loveliest display of winter flowers on his block. He answered, "Plenty of time, Miss."

When their eyes met, he realized she was the woman who took sunrise walks along the narrow Castle Vale streets. He strolled toward her to trade pleasantries, but another man stopped him for a conversation before he could get across the cramped room. At that, Olivia's wandering eyes went to the others standing at the Plexiglas bar, lined with people downing mugs of beer and stronger distillations.

A man with a sallow and wrinkled face puffed on a cigarette that limply hung from the corner of his thin, pink lips. Swirling zephyrs of smoke from the glowing tobacco slowly ribboned upward, evaporating above him and the noisy crowd. His stare was idle as if trapped in a time warp and helplessly stuck at the clattery pub. She thought that it was odd of him to be smoking, seeing that no one else was breaking the rules. Still, there appeared to be no fretting about his lawlessness either. From an angled view, she watched him as his eyes trolled throughout the cacophonous room, transiently fixating on many of the tipsy drinkers. His gaze eventually brushed upon her. But his phlegmatic stare was upended as Olivia shot him a hardened, emotionless look back, so he embarrassingly looked away.

"Can I buy you a beer, Miss?" A musky man with matted gray hair covering most of his face asked gruffly, harassing her and leaning irritatingly close to the point of making unwanted physical contact.

Exposing a semi-toothless smile, he smelled

of pungent liquors and damp, odorous clothes. Although annoyed by the intrusion into Olivis's space, she had watched him hovering over two lone women near the dance floor minutes earlier. Like the others, though, she was prepared to rebuff his advances. One could see that he was wobbling along the stretch of unescorted ladies on his path. He was, needless to say, under the influence of drinking too much.

"No, thank you. I've purchased one already."

Olivia turned away, showing no apology for being irritated by his offensive aggression. With the latter stages of inebriation showing on his badly scared face, he stumbled to the next lady sitting alone further down the bar. The perturbed Professor Reece was relieved that he'd found someone else to bother. The busy bar was overflowing. Patrons huddled near the mahogany walls jammed with shelves of beer mugs, hard liquors, and wines. Others sat alone, sipping contently and observing the happy hour crowd. Soon after, the bartender served her a foam-topped beer on a green coaster that advertised an Irish organic brewery. She casually sipped the barley-flavored liquid while thinking of everything that had to be finished by the next day.

Across the poorly lit room, couples leaned near each other, keeping eavesdroppers from hearing their concupiscent propositions and fabricated promises of love. Such displays of affection caused her to miss Eric and wish for him to be with her.

Minutes later, the phone buzzed at the usual time.

"Hey there, sounds like I'm missing a party."

"Hey, back at you! I'm at a bar not far south of my place. It's pretty crowded here, as you can tell."

Her answer brought concern to him. "You're alone?"

"Yes, I am."

"Is it safe for you to be there by yourself? At night?"

"Oh yeah. I'm ok. Huh? What did you say? Huh? She had trouble hearing him because of the loud bar chatter and booming music.

"Can you hear me?" He asked, shooting up the volume with every word.

"Yes, I heard you. Everything is fine. I won't be here much longer; it is not too dark here yet. I'm cool." She knew his urging was sincere.

"Olivia, are you safe there?."

"I'm about to leave shortly. I promise. Not to worry. I'll use a taxi to get home. I intend to do some work tonight, and I'll leave as soon as I pay my tab. I'll call you when I get in,...and I promise to lock the door behind me," she laughed softly.

"I'm just concerned about you, Sweetie."

"Thanks, Eric, but I'm a big girl. I love you for caring." She said goodbye to him, sipped most of the beer, watched the crowd for another hour, paid five pounds for the drink, and left. The cabstand outside the pub was busy, but she readily caught a ride home.

Olivia continued to settle into her role as a visiting professor, where the students were especially attentive, good-spirited, and hardworking.

Eventually, the date of the International Physics conference in London arrived, and she was eager to see her UST associates.

Olivia's flight to London touched down, and passengers were cleared to leave the cabin. She rushed through the plane's aisle and maneuvered around others exiting into the terminal. Since the flight from Birmingham and the U.S. flight carrying Kip Thibodeaux and William Gibson were arriving around the same time, they agreed to meet at baggage claim before departing for the hotel.

When in the baggage area, she heard William calling out to her. "Hey, Olivia, where is the best bar in this town?" William asked, a smile stretching his cheeks and making his face almost perfectly round. She burst into laughter on seeing them.

"Well, hey there. I can't believe Alexandria Coleman allowed the two of you out of California together! I'll bet UST students are at Garcia's celebrating with their friends right now because their pitiless professors are miles away."

"Whatever!" Kip said, walking ahead of William to give her a bear hug.

After gathering the few pieces of luggage from baggage claim, they took a shuttle to the five-star Albacore Hotel at Whitehall Place and eventually ended up at the pub across from its main lobby.

"William, is this bar okay as a starting point?" Olivia asked, excited to see them.

"We'll see what we can find to top this place after tomorrow's sessions. It'll be no holds barred once we finish setting the audiences on fire," William answered.

"I just want you to stay away from this bar today and be prepared for tomorrow's meeting." Kip laughingly said to him, "Tomorrow's audience might be tough. We still have to get over that bumpy flight coming here, which was nothing to celebrate. At mid-flight, it was hair-raising for us passengers over the Atlantic."

"Really? That's freakin' scary." Olivia said, pursing her lips and sipping more bourbon on the rocks.

"No crap," chimed William.

"How many were on the flight?" She asked curiously.

"I'd say there were at least three hundred," William answered, recalling time in the air. "I sure as hell hope the return is not as bad."

"I see that our sessions tomorrow are two hours apart. The hotel map says I'm four rooms away from you. I'll head over to yours as soon as I'm done," Olivia changed the subject away from the scary flight.

"Great, Olivia. Kip and I will listen in on yours and quietly leave without a disturbance." William winked.

William was usually unassuming at UST and typically moved about campus without fanfare. While here in London, however, he was different. It was a side of William that his friends loved seeing.

"Thanks, Guys," she replied. "I'm glad you'll be there to support me. Hey, I don't want either of you asking crazy-ass questions. Especially you, William."

"I can't promise that." He answered her through chuckles and sips of tonic mixed with gin.

"Right. Try it, my friend. Now, don't you forget what they say about payback." She said to him.

They laughed together, knowing what she meant, and ordered another round.

At least seventy physicists attended Olivia's two-hour session the next day. The crowd was record-setting. Attendees arriving late searched for vacant seats scattered amongst the audience. William and Kip stayed near the rear since they would leave before her session ended. Even so, she was able to see them from the podium. Kip made a supportive thumbs-up gesture, and she nodded with appreciation just before she began.

A well-known physicist, Dr. Stossburg, was the first to ask questions. She'd met him at a previous conference and had spoken with him numerous times about his interest in the Krausberg Theory. He questioned her assertions and solicited examples of purported progress. The exchange, though somewhat superficial, was always cordial. The focus of their respective research was interesting to everyone at the meeting. Afterward, several questions came shooting from the audience.

At the close of the session, Olivia and Dr. Stossburg agreed to stay in touch. She glanced toward the rear of the room where William and Kip had been. As planned, they had already left.

Later, the trio took advantage of the London experience the first evening, hitting a popular restaurant and busy shopping districts. By the end of the three-day conference, they had explored Tower Bridge, Piccadilly Circus, and Westminster Abbey, promising to relive it later over beer and many drinks. Time together allowed them to discuss the interstellar substation and William's conjecture regarding flaws in the spacecraft design.

A rumor was also circulating that Dan Bledsoe was clandestinely consulting with a German-based company, which had been denied participation in the international project. It was believed that Bledsoe was acting as an informant for the company regarding the substation's progress.

By Monday, Professor Reece was back in Birmingham, loaded with new ideas to share with Evelyn and the Birmingham physics department.

The small office on the Birmingham campus with Dr. Garfield was old-fashioned, much like her parent's house full of nineteenth-century antiques. In the tight space, bright sunshine was an intermittent visitor with peeks of it coming through a small window. Still, Olivia liked being there. Sharing the office with Evelyn Garfield was a way of immersing herself in English culture, especially learning much of it from Evelyn.

"Morning, Dr. Reece."

Evelyn pronounced EEEEVELYN, Garfield entered the room and put her handbag on top of the tiny, distressed oak desk nearest the window. The older woman had a desk with a campus view, which marked her faculty seniority status to others.

"Was your night a good one," she cheerfully asked while fluffing her bone-straight shoulder-length hair into place.

"Good morning, Dr. Garfield. My night was ok. I think I'm still recovering from last week's meeting in London. It was well worth it, though. I met many new people. I also spoke with Dr. Stossburg."

Evelyn was wearing a canary yellow dress with a collar trimmed in two rows of black zigzag ribbons. The crisp cotton outfit looked odd, considering it was mid winter. The woman, who favored a famous American pop singer, wore an outfit that made Olivia think of a bumble bee, especially with the black headband against a porcelain white forehead.

"So how was your night?" Olivia asked.

"Oh, it was rather quirky," said Evelyn. "Nice outfit," she continued. Not making much sense of what Evelyn was getting at before thinking, Olivia answered casually,

"Winter in this country is far from what I've known my entire life in California, especially this time of year; oh, and I like what you're wearing, too."

"Thanks," Evelyn said. She straightened her black blazer and fluffed her hair once more. She genuinely liked Evelyn, who was available whenever Olivia needed her. She could pull strings because she was the lead professor in her department. While there, Olivia visited Evelyn's family in Birmingham and attended religious services with her at the historic St. Paul's Church.

"Have you checked your voicemail yet, Olivia?"

"No. Why?"

"I checked mine before getting here. There's a message from Dr. Stossburg. He's inviting us to convene with him and a small group next Thursday. He is most interested in the institutional relationship between Birmingham University and UST."

"What is his real purpose, Evelyn?"

"You can understand what's going on when you check the call, but he wants you to discuss your *Krausberg* study. He's especially interested in your Nano-tech communication theory that's related to quantum entanglement cryptography, particularly since the satellite communications mission was nearly ready to start."

"Okay. I'll call him. However, it should be made clear neither you nor I want to divulge too much too early. What we've done thus far is inconclusive and not yet up for public scrutiny, as you know."

"Absolutely. But I do think the purpose of the meeting is going to be strictly collegial."

"Why yes, of course." Olivia didn't want to sound suspicious. Stossburg, of German descent, was praised globally for his work and was linked to some studies on the *Krausberg Effect*. She'd spoken with him at the London Conference. When they talked briefly after the session, he made her aware of his profound interest in their parallel research. Nevertheless, she had dedicated many years of her life and thousands of lab hours to her interest in Krausberg, work that she didn't want to share with Stossburg.

"You know this could be a high-profile opportunity for you, Olivia," suggested Evelyn. "This is particularly important regarding international communication and security matters." she then said.

Olivia let out a guarded reaction to what Stossburg might be after. "Perhaps that's true."

She wasn't ready to reveal much of her inventive work, especially to him. He couldn't possibly grasp the significance of the hard work she'd invested over the years. Turning away from Evelyn to dial up the

German professor, she said, "Very well. Perhaps I will call him now. I need to know what's going on here."

Stossburg was a graduate of a major university in the United States, and for the most part, was considered a trusted colleague. Regardless of that, she didn't know him well enough to give free rein over the enormous time and study that she'd sacrificed most of her life to achieve. There was no answer at Slossburg's desk, so she left a message for him to return her call.

Evelyn pronounced EEEEVELYN, flaunted a half smile, and commenced sorting papers on her desk while booting up her computer. After the call was made to Stossburg, Olivia considered possible motives driving the sudden request for a meeting. She decided not to discuss her rising concerns with her officemate any further. Before their classes started, the women didn't speak at all.

Thursday, one week later. It was a twenty-minute drive to the hotel conference center, where a meeting with Stossburg and seventeen industrial and university physicists would be convened for a half-day. Evelyn Garfield was behind the wheel and Olivia used the extra time to review the prepared notes.

According to Dr. Stossburg, forty-five minutes was allocated for her to give a brief overview. His directive regarding limited time was well-taken since she purposely intended to hold back on huge chunks of analytics during her talk. When she planned for the meeting days before, she prepared a summary of raw data covering the theory's evolution and her subsequent findings. Most of the information to be presented that day was already a part of her published writings. Defensively, Olivia viewed much of her proprietary work as ongoing and far from conclusive. As such, she did not intend to reveal more of her research than necessary.

The conference center was on the second floor of the century-old Carlyle Hotel on the outskirts of the Birmingham thriving business district. The chandeliered, five-hundred-room resort was opulent, with a cluster of private villas on beautifully landscaped grounds. The grand facility included a lush botanical garden and a large conference complex. Stossburg and Garfield had entered the building to configure the meeting space before the arriving participants.

After getting papers that she inadvertently left in the car, Olivia finally entered the ten-story hotel. In the elevator, the cell phone buzzed.

"Hey there," she was speaking softly to avoid listeners.

"Hello, Babe." Eric said. "I just wanted to hear your voice before boarding the plane. Gotta' go on a one-day consulting run to Houston. I'll be back home later tonight."

Olivia replied, "I'm on my way into the meeting with Dr. Stossburg and Evelyn to go over my recent findings. Do you remember when I brought that meeting up to you?"

"Yes, I remember. You'll be great," he assured her, repeating his confidence.

"Thanks. I'm hoping I'll do alright."

"You will. Besides, if they don't like what you have to say, tell 'em to kiss your...." He stopped short of expressing his opinion and laughed - his voice was seeping through the phone and teasing her with affirming words of love.

She uttered, "You're bad, you know that?"

"Wish I could be bad with you right now."

"I wish you could be, too," still speaking quietly.

"Listen, I'm trying to get there to see you soon. I'm not sure how I can make it happen, but I will. I promise."

She listened, wanting to know more.

"Yeah. I actually may be in Europe for a couple of days soon. Ergowilst wants me in a meeting for them."

"You could make this a mini-vacation with me?"

"Yep, me and you together, all alone. Just us and no one else," he answered.

"You know what, Mr. Blake?" Her voice dropped lower.

"What's that?"

"Wish you were here so I could give you a long, slow kiss for being so bad. Let me know what develops with the possible trip. I want to be extra ready for you when you get here."

"Hearing that makes me wanna' hop on a plane tonight and wake up with you in the morning."

She exited the elevator onto the main corridor toward the conference rooms. "Gotta' say goodbye. I'm about to meet with Evelyn and Dr. Stossburg before the others come."

"I know you'll make us proud today."

Everyone who planned to attend the meeting arrived at the Carlyle except Hans Schweinsteiger from Germany. His company, *Klaus Industrial*, notified Stossburg of his plans not to come. He promised to speak with the professor later in the week and would obtain an update from Boris Sokolov, one of his associates who would be there on his behalf. The other participants, an interesting cast of tech experts and hardcore scholars, also showed up. Olivia knew most of them from their published works or having participated in a few conferences with them.

As soon as she entered the room, Dr. Abigale Francois, a well-regarded physics professor out of France, waved hello from where she chatted with two other women. Most of Olivia's interactions with Dr. Francois were telephonic, although they had previously shared conference panels.

Another familiar face was that of satellite architect Jonathan Fondsbury, the leader of the interstellar substation structural design team. His expertise was in constructing the trillion-dollar component designed to govern global communication. His reputation was the best in his field, where he earned accolades from previous satellite work. Olivia was surprised to see him in attendance but intended to introduce herself to the renowned scientist. Perhaps he could become a trusted ally to advise her on encryption integrity.

In a far corner of the room, three men of Indian heritage sipped hot tea. They appeared to be talking in their native Hindi language, using hand gestures that accented their colorful words.

There were two other men Olivia didn't know. Overhearing them made her assume they were Eastern European nationals, at least judging from the foreign words she heard them speak. As with the Indians, their conversation barely rose above a whisper.

"Good Morning, Ladies and Gentlemen." Dr. Stossburg's pleasant words were a call to begin the meeting. The last quick, hushed greetings were quietly exchanged. He knew everyone there, but importantly, his interest in Olivia's Krausberg study was why he had pulled the group together.

"We can get started now," he said. "We have the room for just four hours, and I want to take full advantage of the space while we are here." His German accent was calming. He was making every effort to clearly communicate with scientists representing many countries.

"By the way," he said, "There is a table with sparkling water and a generous helping of tea biscuits and chocolate chip cookies you may like to have before you sit. I noticed some of you have already helped yourself to the treats to stave off hunger until lunch." Most participants accepted the offer before sitting.

Stossburg and Evelyn were first at the podium. Evelyn introduced herself and her associate, Dr. Stossburg, and then asked participants to give a thirty-second snapshot of their credentials and current research. When the introductions were wrapped up, Stossburg guided the direction of the gathering and urged everyone to adhere to the agenda emailed to them days earlier.

"I want to thank each of you for being here today. This event is monumental, especially when each of you is conducting a lot of independent, inventive work. And to a greater degree, whatever we collectively arrive at today is worthy of furthering with one another in the future. Discussions like these will help to advance our understanding of the much-anticipated substation. Are there any concerns before we get underway?"

At first, no one offered comments. Then one of the men, who traveled from Belarus, Boris Sokolo, asked in broken English, "What timeframe will be for participants to communicate and work together?"

Professor Stossburg answered, "Mr. Sokolov, today will allow us to work with each other to generate new research directions. And some of you may want to walk out of this room and hit the ground running with an idea."

"Hit and run with the idea?" He was confused by the idiomatic choice of words. The group chuckled kindly at the man's innocent misunderstanding. Some people traded humored glances with each other.

"Not run. Not literally. I meant immediately getting started on something two or three of you may have as a shared interest. Something you may have in common."

"Oh, I see." He still didn't quite comprehend what was said - but his response lifted an air of hesitation in the room.

Like others, Olivia was humored by the man's naïveté but didn't pay much attention to the exchange of friendly talk. She was reminiscing Eric's phone call.

"I cannot wait to see him." Her mind dove into thoughts of the man she missed. She intended to call him right after getting back to the condo. She wanted to hear more of his plans to come to Europe.

"Dr. Olivia Reece." Evelyn was calling her to the panelist table. For a brief second, the American professor was lost in thoughts of Eric and an intimate time with him at her place in California. Her reserved smile was like a window into her secret daydream.

Evelyn asked again. "Dr. Reece, are you ready?"

"Oh yes. Thank you, Dr. Garfield."

With that, Olivia approached the head table to begin.

After about forty minutes of divulging general details about her theoretical work, there came at least a dozen questions in search of more information. Days later, participants' feedback would judge her discussion as overwhelmingly good.

Later that night, Castle Vale was quiet when Eric called to say good night. Although Olivia was already in bed, it wouldn't have mattered what the clock showed. She hadn't called earlier as promised because of a tight schedule but was excited to get his call.

"When will you be coming here?" She was already creating lustful scenarios in her head.

"Humm. Don't quite know yet, but much sooner than you think."

She closed her eyes and imagined their last time together before leaving for Europe. More than ever, she missed him.

The next day, during the early morning hours, she wrote a heartfelt letter to him.

My Dearest Eric,
There is so much I must learn about experiencing real love
and the enjoyment of connecting with someone as
wonderful as you. For the very first time, I understand the

true meaning of the adage "love is not selfish". You see, now I don't wish only for what I want in this relationship but what WE can DO to ensure the purest love between us. Your love for me is solely your choice, but I want to be sure I honor and appreciate the goodness you are willing to give - I'm so proud of being yours. Yes, Eric, you have carved an unforgettable mark of love on my heart. I will treasure all we share in this new and exciting togetherness and take good care of the love you're giving me each day. I'm yours.

Olivia.

Chapter 16
Confirmation

Until now, it had been a predictable pattern. Whenever Olivia's guard dropped in past relationships, insecurity overshadowed her heart's confidence. Even when she tried her best, she couldn't control the doubts that swayed her fragile emotions. Her hesitancy to open up to real love often occurred without her expecting it. It was a way of protecting her heart. On the other hand, Eric seemed different, and his devotion to her was proving to be unmistakably genuine.

"How are you this morning, Olivia?"

She no longer hid her joy whenever they talked or when together.

"Got some good news for you" he said.

"What is it?"

"What I promised you last week has come true. I've got a flight to Barcelona in a few days. I'm going to meet with Ergowilst's European partner, Klaus Industrial to help them with designing updated cockpits and passenger seating floor plans. It is short notice since they will be in Barcelona briefly. I was not about to miss the chance to see you," Eric said.

Germany-based Klaus Industrial, known for its hurry-up production operations, built small planes, spacecraft, satellite equipment, and cockpit simulators for European and Asian clients. Klaus wanted to expand its clientele globally, including the U.S. Olivia squealed. "That is great! That's awesome, Baby! "

He coaxed her, "Have you missed me? Have you?"

"Of course, I have."

"Why don't you tell me how much you've missed me," She didn't respond at first, still reveling in the exciting news.

"I'm waiting, Professor." He urged her to tell him.

"I miss you so much. I get all hot and bothered when I think of you."

She evenly let her loneliness be known, teasing his imagination as she spoke.

"I miss you so much that a cold bath is never cold enough to cool my desires, even when the air conditioner blasts and ice covers me from head to toe in the tub."

"How much more?" he encouraged.

"Eric, I've missed you so much that… that I've…that I've…"

She stopped the lustful monologue and changed the subject. "Well, Mr. Lucky Man, how did you manage to get a trip to Spain?"

"That was so unfair, Olivia Reece," he pleaded. "Why did you stop there? I was lost in that steamy scene you created for me."

"Please tell me how you pulled off coming to Europe. Or must I punish you for not telling me when you come here?"

He gave in to her ultimatum. "Adrianna Brown, an Ergowilst engineer, is managing a project in Sacramento and needed to finish the job, so I will come to Spain in her place."

"That's terrific."

"I'm arriving there next Tuesday on Flight 807 and arriving at 3:30 P.M., local time. The good thing is that I added a couple of days to the trip for us. I'm free for two days before I meet with the Ergowilst client. Pretty sweet, huh?"

"Yes, that's very cool," she answered. Later that night, her phone beeped while working on final edits to a lecture. It was early in the U.S. but minutes before midnight in England. The device showed a text message from Eric that revealed his yearning. She smiled as she read and responded. "Hello, my beautiful Olivia."

"Hey there!"

"Love you."

"Love u back!" She replied with a "good night" and a promise to be waiting for his call as usual. Eric called Olivia the next day.

"Got a lot to tell you when I see you! This place is unbelievable! I've had a chance to see a lot, and I want to take you to every place I've been."

"Yeah. I want to see everything, too, as long as you're with me. But two days won't be enough time to do that, Olivia." He gently responded to her.

"Yes, I suppose you're right."

She answered back. "We can do that together one day," he promised.

He listened to her go on about England and while listening, thought of life for them together... married. But he was dwelling in thoughts of the touchy conversation with his mother.

He had to admit that, in many ways, his mother had been on point. Even so, he held on to regret about how she'd brought up not having grandchildren. In his mind, what mattered most was how he decided to direct his own life, not what his mother needed in hers.

Although he wasn't sure of what a condition of matrimony might ultimately bring, he loved Olivia enough to consider it. He was sure she loved him, too. However, it would be devastating if she rejected his confession of wanting her as his wife. What if she said no? What if that happened? What if he would be more disappointed than in the past? He was not ready to endure that level of hurt. At least not then. He'd fallen into thought about their relationship while Olivia was still raving about his upcoming arrival in Europe.

"What do you think? Do you want me to go there? Meet you in Barcelona?" She proposed the idea as an option.

"Would that make it easier on you, Eric?"

"Don't know, Babe. Possibly."

"With my schedule, I can take a break from the university and fly there instead of your coming to Birmingham after you get to Spain."

"I'm not sure. I have to think about it." His mother's biased comments were still crowding his mind.

"And... my Love, when you get here, I'll need way more than just one night of delicious and sweet lovemaking with you."

All at once, Olivia's provocative words pulled an answer from him. "Okay," he said. "Fair enough. With a promise like that, I can't argue with you. I'll have a ticket for you at the airport in Birmingham, Sweetheart. Meeting me in Spain works. I want to make the most of our short time together."

"Me, too. I can take three days off. My assistant can manage the sessions in the lab without me," said Olivia. "Plus, I want to see other parts of Europe before returning home. This trip will be one of them."

"That's a good idea," he answered her.

She responded naughtily, "Yeah. But right now, I just want to be with you."

"Needing you more," he insisted while appreciating Olivia's longing to be with him.

"Will you meet with your client as soon as you arrive?"

"Nope. First, I'll have forty-eight hours to myself. No problem at all."

"Great! We can meet at the airport. Should I reserve a hotel for us?"

"Thanks, Sweetheart. There is no need for you to do any of that. I'll take care of everything. I'll call you with more details tomorrow."

"I'll be waiting," she said, wanting the conversation to go on forever. They would be together in a couple of days.

Just beyond where she stood in the overflowing Barcelona airport, winter's cold winds whistled through icy doors that automatically open for travelers going to their final destinations. Strong gusts intermittently tossed Olivia's hair about her face while she waited in the cavernous baggage claim area. The chill caused her to pull the leather jacket tighter as the frigid European air swirled into the building. Luckily, she'd decided to wear a thick lamb's wool sweater to keep warm.

The nippy conditions didn't matter to her. She was not about to move from her location since she didn't want the slightest chance of missing him. Not long now, she would be with Eric.

She checked her watch every five seconds and then rechecked it as the time closed in on his arrival; she was anxious.

Passengers came down the slow-moving escalator, but there was no sign of him. Waiting was painstaking. She was afraid to take her eyes away from the escalator cranking its way down to the ground floor. Olivia eagerly surveyed the crowd of travelers towing wheeled bags behind them. Had she somehow missed him? There was no sign of him.

An uneasiness was setting in and she couldn't dispense it. Had flight plans changed without any notice? Some unforeseen trouble with the plane? Olivia became more concerned as she waited.

Then she saw him. Her knees buckled as he stepped off the escalator and rushed to their rendezvous. When he caught a glimpse of her, she could see his perfect, pearl-white smile as his pace accelerated to where she was waiting. The uncontrolled pounding in her chest brought on by the sight of him was irrepressible, and a state of nervousness and excitement completely seized her. Before she knew it, she was rushing, virtually running his way.

The resurgence of desire intensified as the man she adored rushed by people to reach her. At that moment, a voice inside reminded Olivia of how she had been lonely for months without him. She believed that was also true for him. As he neared her, a flood of good memories - of every special moment together- came over her. She knew then that he was right for her.

When he finally reached her, there was no concern for who might be watching. He caught her around the waist, lifted her, and pressed a long, tender kiss on a mouth he'd missed. Olivia's eager heart turned molten, allowing herself to take in the moment of having his mouth on hers and being with him again. And in the same way, his loving eyes confessed what he held inside.

"Let's get outta' here," he suggested, enfolding her hand with his. They were ready to be alone.

Outside on the curb, a string of taxi cabs waited to scoop up impatient travelers hurrying to leave the airport. Eric beckoned for a car, which sped ahead of two others, seizing the couple from the band of competing cabbies. The driver jumped out and greeted them first in Spanish, then in English.

Advanced fluency in Spanish and German had helped Eric land many contracts with Ergowilst. It guaranteed an excellent payout for his company whenever he partnered with them on a European contract. So when they needed someone to work with foreign clients, Velocity was called. He casually gave the taxi driver the hotel's name in Spanish and confirmed the rate to get them there. The driver was happy to comply.

They climbed onto the back seat holding hands, unwittingly ignoring admiring onlookers. The driver was enthusiastic about chauffeuring the American couple, so he told them he'd pass through the city's urban center and then down coastal roads to the beach. He added that the ride to the hotel would take a half hour.

Like the most of Spain, Barcelona was fondly known for its uncompromising rush hour traffic. The constant flow of cars typically persisted throughout the day. On this day, mounting congestion in the heart of the city was caused by traffic-choking vehicles that made taxi passengers painfully aware of the bumps and frequent potholes on poorly paved streets. Anyone captured in city traffic could only wish their final stop was much closer.

"The flight here was a little bumpy," she said. "I couldn't help but think about the first time we were together, and the bed was bumpy, too."

He put his eyes lovingly on her, showing his desires, and whispered back, "Sí. Algo realmente especial ocurrió entre nosotros esa noche y nunca, nunca lo lamenté." ("Yes. Something really special happened between us that night and I have never, ever regretted it."

He didn't speak much more during the drive to the hotel, but Eric's heart and mind were fixed on the woman next to him. He wrapped his arm around her for reassurance that the moment was real.

His head rested on her shoulder as he whispered, "It was an uncomfortable flight. I think it had a lot to do with a crying baby in the coach cabin. Even though I was in Business Class trying to review my notes for the meeting, I could hear it fussing. It was hard for me to concentrate. Imagine that?"

She could hear hints of annoyance. "Why do you say that?"

"I'm glad I was not the flight captain."

"Oh?"

"Yeah." He lazily answered, allowing his body to meld into hers. "Would have been a helluva' lot different if I'd been captain. I would have asked the parents to quiet that kid. Better yet, what if I had been that kid's dad?"

Olivia's reaction was blithesome. "Watch out Mr. Tough Guy. You're scaring me."

"You'd better believe it, my Sista'." He said, from lips that showed the charming smile she loved. "If it had been my kid it would've been an angel the whole time. It would have been a happy baby on the entire flight."

She remembered what his mother said about him starting a family and thought of him as being a good father.

He said, "Yep, I'm ready for two days with you. And I won't let you out of my sight for one minute." He held her for the third deliciously slow kiss.

"Yes, indeed." She flirted with eyes on him, finding it easy to lean into the sexual energy they were sharing.

The dusty, dinged-up black sedan wheeled into the hotel's main entrance, where eager employees competed for hefty tips. The cab stopped at the gold-framed revolving entrance, where a doorman wearing a neatly pressed red and tan uniform waited to greet them.

The enthusiastic driver stated the fare. It was reasonable. Eric paid the money and included an extra forty dollars in U.S. currency. After the transaction, he asked the Spaniard if he could reserve a trip back to the airport. He'd need the ride for Olivia in two days. The young man, with unusually long, slick, jet-black sideburns and glossy slick black hair, gladly complied with his request. He handed his American passenger a business card and reiterated that he would take care of them. After indicating approval of the promise, Eric took the two pieces of luggage, and the couple entered the hotel.

They were pleasantly struck once in the lobby of the high-end *Hotel Grande Torre*, which resembled a castle dating as far back as the Fourteenth Century. Eric showed her replicas of paintings done by famous Spanish artists that were galleried in the hotel lobby. Their names were easily pronounced, suggesting he knew a lot about them. She'd only heard of one Spanish artist among them, but he casually talked of each artist as if he'd studied them with genuine interest.

The hotel's Medieval architecture was an impressive impersonation of buildings that existed centuries before the couple was born. They talked about what it must have been like to live in Europe in the past and how they would have been oblivious to today's modern culture. After registering, they boarded the elevator to the twelfth floor.

The suite was immaculate; two lavishly ornate chairs and an elegant king-sized bed with a headboard of the finest Bojonegoro Teak dominated the room. Undoubtedly pleased with the couple's reaction to the superior accommodation, the friendly bellman detailed the hotel amenities in broken English. He recommended various must-see places in the city, then gratefully said goodbye after accepting a substantial tip.

Eric latched the door and watched her move about the suite in child-like curiosity. She peered from a window, looking down at the congested streets. Hundreds of shoppers, mainly tourists saddled with packages, scurried on the busy sidewalks.

One man in a gray woolen sweater and matching scarf pushed his way through people waiting to enter a symphony hall across the narrow street. A crowd was forming near the door, and a woman appeared to shoot a puzzled look at the man wearing the bulky sweater while sharply reacting to his boorishness. Amid the chaos, the woman pointed her finger at what might have been a marquee posting the business hours. He didn't notice her. Or, possibly, didn't give a damn that he was offending her with rude behavior. Everyone else ignored him entirely and huddled closer to the doorway, hoping to escape the cold and find warmth in the breezeway.

The professor's gaze wandered to a ferry docked at the waterfront. The double-decker vessel with a group of young partygoers ignored the wintry conditions. It was an evening cruise taking off from Icaria Beach. She imagined nippy conditions onboard because blustery gales stormily pounded the medium-sized boat. The gusts were brisk as the vessel rocked from rough, lashing winds, making the passengers seek balance by holding onto the promenade balusters.

"You like what you see?"

"Wow, Eric. This place is something. Why don't more people come to Barcelona?"

He didn't readily reply, watching her every move, thinking only of the innocent joy she was showing.

"Don't know. Maybe we're the ones who didn't know

about this city, Sweetheart."

He walked across the ornate rug, past the Mediterranean-style chairs in front of the eight-foot crystalline windows overlooking the city, beyond the bed, and stopped next to Olivia. When near her, he was able to breathe in her loveliness. His lungs had missed the fragrance of her perfume, and he ached for the comfort of her buttery-soft skin every time he woke up alone in the middle of the night. Finally, he was with her.

Being in a relationship with her during the last months had helped to extinguish any thoughts of wanting to remain single, and he was starting to want to be with her even more. Fulfillment touched him in that revealing moment, and he was happy.

She looked at him and said lovingly, "I'm hungry. Are you?"

"Yeah, I sure am, for many delicious things," he answered with a trace of mischievous flavor in his voice. "But let's get out of here, find some good Spanish food, and check out Barcelona for a while. You game for that?"

"Okay."

Charmed by his attention, she brushed her shapely, round hips against him and tenderly traced her finger across his forearm before pulling on her coat. "Let's go," she said.

Just as they were about to head out the door, Eric's phone rang. He answered the caller in German. "Hey, what's up Hans? Yeah, I made it here two hours ago. Okay. Meet you there at 9:30. Bye."

He sighed and said, "Now, where were we? Were you talking about wanting to eat... or?"

She quietly laughed at his innuendo and responded, "I think we were talking about treating ourselves to some Spanish food. Shall we go?"

Barcelona was new to them, and their time together was planned to be unforgettable. They took the advice of the hotel concierge about where to eat and rode the underground Metro de Barcelone public transportation system instead of taking a cab. The plan was to dive into the city's culture and nightlife for the next forty-eight hours.

They started with a stop at *Can Culleretes*, the second oldest restaurant in Spain – opening its doors to hungry Spaniards in 1786. The classic Catalan down-home place served wild boar stew, pork sausage with white beans, seafood pica, and authentic paella. The wild boar would be too far on the edge for her, but Eric's curious palate enticed him to try it, and he liked it.

After a second day of exploring Barcelona, her early morning departure was just hours away. Back in the hotel on the second night, they prepared for her to leave early the next morning, just before dawn. For several minutes, everything in the room was muted. She packed silently, and he confirmed with the hotel concierge that the reserved taxi would take her to the airport as agreed.

He broke the silence, looking into eyes that pooled with tears. "It won't be long before you're back in California with me." He drew her to his chest, and she felt the warmth of his love.

"The time spent with you outweighs any price," she whispered up at him.

Two days in the city had turned out to be sensual love, filled with playful, libidinous moments for the couple: walking on the beach at dusk, impromptu sexy salsa dancing at the fashionable Mondo Club, sipping bottles of Spanish red wine at the famous Harlem Jazz Club and making bold, indiscreet, noisy and lustful love once back in the hotel room.

On that last night, he wanted to spend every waking moment showing Olivia how much he cared and would miss her until they were together again.

Eric's meeting with Klaus Industrial ended on the second day at one o'clock. Boris Sokolov, who was present at the quickly organized Stossburg meeting in Birmingham, was also in the Barcelona meeting.

Right after Eric left to pack for departure, Sokolov met privately with Hans to provide an update. He reported that at the Birmingham meeting, Professor Reece had laid out details about how her study might benefit the interstellar substation launch and how it would be a global communications game-changer. Boris also believed the professor had deliberately narrowed the *Krausberg* Effect discussion to already publicly known information. He suggested to Hans that being there was a waste of his time. They needed another means of getting the critical data from her. More importantly, because of Klaus' business ties with other questionable countries, they had been excluded from submitting a proposal to participate in the interstellar project.

Before leaving the meeting with Hans Schweinsteiger, owner of Klaus Industrial, Boris was told, "I think Dan Bledsoe can help us because he worked with Reece at UST and would likely know her travel schedule. Do whatever is necessary as long as it does not come back to me or my company. This is strictly between us."

Meanwhile, Eric's flight to California would take off at 11:00 P.M., and he needed to rest before leaving Spain. When riding the taxi to the hotel, he called Olivia to update her on his return itinerary. He was due back in Los Angeles around 4:00 P.M. the next day. His plan was to call her as soon as he was home.

Hours after a much-needed power nap in the Barcelona hotel, he was boarding a plane for the United States.

While flying home, Eric wrote:

Olivia, My Love, I cannot explain why my heart longs for you, and why these feelings are so incredibly strong. But what I know is that you've repaired my broken soul and you've given me all that I've missed with others. You healed every wound of sadness and replaced the hurt with your amazing love. They say time heals all wounds. I'm grateful to have found you to help heal them for me.

With All My Love, Eric

The next few months in England passed quickly. Olivia's remaining time meant conducting and formalizing routine research with the faculty under the leadership of Professor Evelyn Garfield. On one occasion, Dr. Garfield mentioned cautions about the Stossburg meeting participants, indicating some shouldn't have been there. Nonetheless, she did not speak of the meeting again. Meanwhile, the Krausberg investigation consumed Olivia. All the while, she achieved her goals. Notably, she finished the encryption formulation. The highly sensitive asset was to be known exclusively by a select few, including Drs. Thibodeaux and Gibson.

PART THREE

Chapter 17
Home

The evening in September was balmy, and the air was thick with typical Southern humidity when the plane started its final descent to the East Coast International Airport. Flight attendants passed through the main cabin, reminding passengers to prepare for landing. More than three hundred travelers comprised the lengthy flight manifest, with many foreigners entering the U.S. for the first time.

There had been a misty shower before the A380 jetliner rumbled downward and slowly glided over the glassy, rain-soaked airstrip. The familiar bump and loud screech of the aircraft tires brought sighs of relief from weary passengers glad to be on the ground. Moments later, the plane finally stopped at the designated terminal gate awaiting their arrival. Olivia adjusted her seat, freshened her lipstick, and thought of being home and seeing her family after such a long time.

Distracted by the slowed exit, two children sitting behind her noisily played with one another in games that were repeated over and over for four thousand miles. The younger child annoyingly kicked the back of Olivia's seat as the other youngster flipped the armrest and looped the Mary Had a Little Lamb lyric, irritating everyone in earshot.

Once passengers were standing to debark, a reminder to be careful when opening overhead bins was announced. Olivia tugged at her rollaboard and, although fatigued by the long flight, soon dislodged it from the cramped space above her seat.

Fortunately, she had already shipped some belongings days before. One small piece of luggage would be waiting for her at Customs.

In the aircraft's narrow aisle, a long-haired teenager frowned because of Olivia's slower pace, shifting his welterweight, pencil-like body and slicing her with his steel-gray eyes. She politely ignored his adolescent restlessness and moved as quickly as she could. Even with the difficulty of juggling her luggage, she quickly joined the flow of exhausted passengers who all wanted to exit.

While waiting to leave, her thoughts drifted to Eric. When she left for England months earlier, they knew being away from one another would be difficult. They believed it would be a test of commitment to making the relationship work. Nonetheless, they needed time and space to sort out their feelings for one another.

Without mistake, Eric needed to get past Jasmine, who tarnished his faith in ever having a meaningful relationship. He had finally begun to realize that the sting of his past love disaster had embittered him to emotional impotence. Eric left his ex, never wanting romantic love to be a part of him again. He'd been lonely since breaking up with Jasmine and needed change. He was also beginning to realize he wanted to experience a change with Olivia. And at the same time, Olivia's insecurities had kept her from loving freely. Eric brought honest love into her life. It was an evolving dignity that promised mature happiness for them. For the both of them it felt right.

As she waited, passenger conversations in the cabin were getting louder. The impatient chatter brought Olivia back from her thoughts to where she was then standing. At this point, everyone was bunched in the aisles with centimeters of space between them in the uncomfortably narrow space. A tall woman answered her phone while speaking German to the caller."Hallo, wir sind hier! Es war eine gute Reise! Wie geht es dir" ("Hello. We are here! It was a good trip! How are you?").

The person on the other end of the call said something and the German woman spoke again.

"Es tut mir leid, dass Sie eine Erkältung haben und sich nicht gut fühlen. Ich werde Sie wieder anrufen, wenn wir das Hotel zu erreichen. Auf Wiedersehen." (I'm sorry you have a cold and are not feeling well. I will call you again when we reach the hotel. Goodbye.

While Olivia could not understand the woman, her speaking in German called forth, in Olivia's mind, the mysterious meeting with the Stossburg group at the Carlyle Hotel. Some of the participants showed a peculiar interest in her encryption formulations, none of which she divulged.

She remembered that when she entered the Carlyle conference room that morning, she overheard Evelyn suggesting that Olivia meet Hans Schweinsteiger and Klaus Industrial representatives to discuss her theories.

But when they realized that she was nearby, the conversation changed. Nor was it brought up at any time later with Evelyn.

From the beginning, she had misgivings about the meeting that brought others to meet with Stossburg in

Birmingham. The Belarus nationals, in particular, asked pointed questions about encryption techniques and how the work of UST physicists would contribute to the substation security. Though she trusted Evelyn, something about the gathering still felt wrong. She needed more answers and would go after them now back at UST.

Travelers on the flight began the familiar routine: gather their baggage, wait, move toward the exit, wait, and then dash through the boarding bridge and into the terminal. In this case, all travelers had to clear Customs first. The process would likely be slow and cumbersome as thousands of flights enter the country daily. She expected to spend at least thirty to forty minutes creeping through the first phases of returning home.

Fortunately, a short time later, the first reentry hurdle was faster than expected, and with the passport cleared, Olivia jumped into gear toward the next departure gate. After spending so much time in the air, she didn't want to miss her connection to Los Angeles since there were still four and a half hours to go.

With her carry-on tote on her shoulder and towing the matching rollaboard, Olivia rushed around hundreds of passengers and took the first shuttle leaving Customs. All she wanted was to get to Terminal C and gate C-36. The gate was the last one in the remotely located terminal.

Once off the overcrowded shuttle, she rushed toward the nearest escalators, where a mass of passengers dashed behind her, all headed in the same direction.

On the top of the stairs, she saw a sign for Terminal C, which revealed gate C-36 was still some distance away.

The moderately busy terminal was the typical airport commercial zone: long corridors of shops and fast-food vendors. Despite growing hunger, getting to the gate was at the top of Olivia's mind. Soon after covering more distance in the terminal, her pace slowed; C-36 was nearby.

Chapter 18
Perpetrators

Pop!...Pop!... Pop! The quick popping sounds exploded throughout the broad corridor near gate C-36. She checked the time on her phone. It was 7:15 P.M.

"It's probably an equipment malfunction," assumed Olivia. Despite that, the sounds unnerved her, and she soon sensed something was terribly wrong. She looked around the terminal entrance for signs of possible danger. By this time, her worries were real; the amplified popping happened again.

Pop! Pop! Pop! The loud popping matched the clap of gunfire. It numbed her, and she feared approaching danger. Alarmed travelers ran away from the terrifying explosions. Hundreds fled the terminal, desperately seeking safety. Terror-stricken toddlers clung to their parents and abandoned toys in the wake of a frightening and pandemonic scene.

"What on earth is going on?" Olivia panicked. "There is something wrong here! Oh shit!! What the hell is happening? What is going on?" Like everyone else around her, she was afraid. The echo of gunfire was heard in the building as the shooting accelerated. Then came more thunderous quick popping sounds; this time, it was closer to her!

"Oh, God," Olivia thought, "This is serious!" She looked around for a means to protect herself.

She needed to find the nearest safe place to fashion a defense. Then, after seeing crowds rushing into restrooms to block the open entrances, she ran in another direction, fearing the risk would be much too high if they hid together in a single location. Another explosion occurred. This one was within yards.

"Gotta' think! I've got to think quickly!"

Near the departure gate, there was a stainless-steel storage unit. The large compartment was flung wide open, likely caused when people rushed to safety. She hurried toward the empty unit because the dangerous situation called for quick action.

A pair of male voices came in her direction. They were speaking with familiar Eastern European intonations. Slovakia, Hungary, or Romania perhaps? She recognized the inflections and cadences of the words but couldn't translate them.

"I got to freakin' hurry! Where did everyone else disappear to? Where did airport workers hide? What is happening?"

Had she missed an airport warning, like others hiding in terminal C? She didn't know. But in that frightening moment, she had to find safety. Her life was at stake.

She pushed her rollaboard farther away, sending it toward abandoned luggage scattered in the nearly empty terminal. She didn't want her belongings to cause any suspicion of her presence. A few others, caught up in the mayhem, dashed for whatever cover they could find.

She had to hide. Now in a state of horror, she squeezed into the tight metal storage space that turned into her hideaway. There was barely enough room to shut it but small ventilation slats could be seen above her. Neiter did she have any sort of weapon to protect herself, since no form of weaponry was allowed in the airport facility.

Luckily, Olivia silenced her phone on the plane and forgot to turn the ringer on when she texted her parents and Eric from Customs. Seconds later, what sounded like someone speaking Russian could be heard. Olivia gripped the handle tightly, fearing her movement inside the steel compartment would threaten her safety.

"Are you sure this is the terminal she was supposed to be in?"

"Yes. According to my cousin Olga, who works here, this is the one. She checked the passenger list. But I haven't seen anyone that fits that description."

"She is a black woman, Dr. Olivia Reece. Black, curly hair. I've seen her before. Her flight came from England on World Airlines A380," another said, speaking Russian.

Although Olivia could not understand their language or figure out what they were saying, she heard the name Olivia Reece. They were looking for her. "What the hell can they want with me!"

"Have you checked this area thoroughly, Boris?" A man, again speaking Russian, asked.

"Yes, it looks clear. I checked the first pair of restrooms, and they are empty," Boris confirmed.

The lead Russian gave stern commands to the other two accomplices as they approached where she hid.

What if they find her? She had to remain calm; otherwise, exposure might've become a hostage situation. As they neared her, Olivia searched her memory of why she'd missed warnings of an attack or, for that matter, why they were interested in her.

Unaware of the proximity to their target, Boris stationed himself within steps of Olivia's hideout. The semi-automatic weapon slung across his shoulder turned excruciatingly heavy. So, for a brief minute, the Russian propped the gun on the tall stainless storage box behind him with the barrel of the weapon pointing upward. Olivia was inside the container, and the pinging sound of the gun hitting her secret place unsettled her. Could he suspect she was in there? Was his location a ploy to draw her out? The darkness made the situation incomprehensible.

The attackers had taken control of one area in the international building after airport workers of Russian descent helped them. Olga Romanov and Peter Petrov permitted the co-assailants to sneak loaded guns and pounds of explosives into Terminal C. They concealed the contraband underneath clothing in luggage that was cleverly shielded from scanners and smuggled the weapons through an employee clearance gate.

Olivia was not aware that the assailants comprised one woman and eight men. Three were stationed near her, and six more had momentarily shut down airport security at the main entrance of Terminal C. She had no idea the East European assailants were after control of the interstellar substation planned for global orbit in several weeks.

While she didn't know why they were interested in her unpublished work, they were aware that nanotechnology enables nanonetworks to interface with communication links and manipulate communication remotely. Being in control of Krausberg's research and the encryptions she'd successfully developed would give the Russian conspirators a commanding advantage of critical scientific formulations over competing nations such as the United States and its allies. Her conclusive work with Krausberg's research would likely strengthen the global dominance that this group of perpetrators were going after.

"How insane of them to think they could hold an entire airport hostage, especially one of international value. There's too much security protecting this facility." But for now, she could only wait in fear of being discovered and possibly losing her life. Time ticked.

The situation spiked, and everything changed suddenly. The three culprits, possibly Russian, talked while trying to find Olivia, yet had no clue she was nearby.

"Viktor, Dmitry, come here! Come here! Come now!" Boris waved his hands frantically and signaled the two men dressed in stolen airport employee uniforms. He wanted them to leave their posts and come in his direction.

"What is wrong, Boris?" One of the men asked, looking puzzled and anxious.

"I think someone is still hiding in this area. I have not seen anyone, but I believe I am right."

"What makes you so sure?" another asked. Boris' answer was emphatic.

"Maybe it is just a strange feeling, but it is a very strong one!"

"Oh, you are foolish! You are just thinking out of your head, Boris."

The Russian who had been quiet thus far asked. "Have you checked in all the food places as you were supposed to?"

"Yes. Yes, of course!" Boris was put off with Dmitry's lack of trust. "I told you this was a bad idea! This place has armed security everywhere! I wish we had waited to take her in California but Hans insisted we move quickly with Dr. Bledsoe's help."

"Stop talking and come with us now. We must search again. And again. If someone is here, we will find them!"

"Your plan is not working, Dimitry! I don't like it."

"They're foreign operatives," Olivia determined.

Flashbacks of Reece's meeting with Dr. Stossburg at the Carlyle Hotel came upon her. She had recollections of the two Russians from Belarus who were in attendance that day. They'd asked many questions about atmospheric navigational conditions and how she might successfully bind her theoretical work with the space station systems. Her brief answers recommended that they conduct more inquiries into the functions of flight instruments. Their roles as agents of German-based Klaus Industrial were unknown at that time. As intended, many aspects of her proprietary research were intentionally omitted, and the time the Russians spent at the Stossburg Birmingham meeting was fruitless.

When at the Carlyle Hotel, Olivia wanted to believe there was respect for intellectual property. However, it appears that the two men had ulterior motives. If her hunch was correct, the attackers in terminal C knew what the participants had discussed.

Thoughts of that meeting stopped when another Russian, who was likely the lead perpetrator, neared her hiding place and commanded the others to follow him. Viktor, Dmitry, and Boris left their posts with weapons ready. Together, they methodically searched the area, opening doors and peering beneath tables pushed into corners and storage spaces that had been overlooked during the first search. Prayers helped Olivia. The men failed to find her as they searched for her.

Shattered glass that didn't hit the floor at the first explosion crashed onto the tile. The noise distracted the culprits' tedious walk-through. Seeing no proof that a lone passenger hid nearby, Viktor told Dmitry and Boris to return to their assigned posts.

The lead Russian spoke to someone else in another part of the terminal, ensuring the area was clear. Suddenly, communication among the assailants ceased. After cursing loudly in Russian, he slammed the phone to the floor, telling cohorts he wasn't sure of how they would continue to communicate. Federal authorities had shut down all area cell towers.

Boris, the gangly, six-foot-five man moved back to his assigned spot and remained a few steps from Olivia. He adjusted his heavy weapon, tightening the wide black strap. As soon as he straightened the gun, another loud boom rocked the terminal, and the tinkling of shattered glass was heard in restaurants and vending areas. Boris took more steps backward, again coming within inches of her. Now watchfully pacing back and forth, the awkward Russian repeatedly bumped the steel door, not knowing it hid the woman he was after.

Terminal C was under full attack. She counted at least four men near her, but a few more were likely elsewhere. Not knowing what might be happening in other locations of the international complex, Olivia could only pray that she remained alive. Her worries were growing at warp speed.

"Help! Is anyone out there? We need help!"

A woman cried out in the terminal and a Russian ran toward the urgent plea. He jerked a bathroom stall door open and discovered a mother and small child cowering inside. The man pressed his finger against his lips and said, "Quiet. Quiet!" He pushed the door shut and walked away.

An uncanny hush loomed and steeled the terminal. More silence. The silence troubled Olivia, who prayed for signs of help coming soon. Her cautious judgment supposed an empty and shattered area with no one else there - except for a few passengers held at gunpoint and the Russians who'd taken control of the airport's northwest quadrant.

The echo of a big man's shoes pacing the hard floor made her uneasy. Several times, the attacker came scarily close to discovering her. It was harder and harder to breathe as she prayed to be rescued from the steel box.

At the end of what seemed like the longest two hours, the circumstances dramatically changed; the dangerous situation ended, sparing the lives of many innocent airport passengers. The polished precision of law enforcement impressively swept the area, captured the Russians, and brought safety to the terminal. Federal agents arrested the Russians without harm to others, including the frightened woman and child in

Terminal C. There was one exception, however: the Russian named Boris was caught without his weapon and attempted to flee. Consequently, gunfire caught him in the torso. The swift action carried out by SWAT tactical forces successfully put the Russian culprits in federal custody.

By an apparent miracle, the siege did not escalate to a deadly scenario. Olivia, too, emerged from the tight hiding place without a scratch. Authorities escorted her to a questioning room before releasing her.

The bandits had wanted to force her into revealing the encryption key data. This crew of bungling U.S. adversaries believed the key would grant them access to every institution of significant value worldwide. Fortunately, their efforts, even with the help of Dan Bledsoe, had not worked.

Later that week, following the aftermath, the amateurish takeover was suppressed by news reporters and hidden from the breaking news headlines. Olivia was protected from the media spotlight, avoiding speculation from conspiracy theorists, and NASA remained guarded about the information it released to the public. Meanwhile, federal authorities planned to investigate the incident in secrecy, including the guilt of Dan Bledsoe, who aided the Russians with information obtained from UST. The physicist had used his association with the UST physics department to curry favors with the assailants. He was arrested later for having ties with Sokolov. His vendetta against UST and the work of Reece, Thibodeaux, and Gibson had failed. Meanwhile, it would take months for officials to repair structural damage to the terminal and process forensic evidence collected at gate C.

Two days following the airport incident, Eric called Olivia and offered to bring breakfast. She wanted to rest but also needed his care. She wanted him to come by.

Quietly, he let himself in through the front door. She was sleeping well, and he hesitated to wake her. He stood in her bedroom entrance for a few minutes and watched her rest. The bedroom was messy, littered with a half-empty suitcase, pieces of clothing she'd worn on the flight, and other possessions brought with her from England. Daylight was trying to enter; except for that, the room was dim.

He whispered her name. "Olivia, Olivia, it's me." Awakened by his familiar voice, she could see a blurred image of him that conveyed concern for her. With rumpled hair, she looked tired, her face devoid of makeup.

"It's ten in the morning. How are you feeling," he asked, wanting clues about her state of mind.

"Morning, Eric. I'm doing okay. I'm sorry I didn't hear you come in," she said, still clinging to slumber.

"Yeah. No problem. You were resting."

"I'm glad you're here. I was dreaming of you," she rose from the bed.

He sat next to her and patiently listened. "You wanna' tell me about the dream?"

"The dream was a little confusing, but we were somewhere...I think it was on a beach...I don't know... I know we were together."

He pulled her nearer. She caressed his shoulder and whispered, "I need you closer to me right now."

A tsunami of longing swept over the couple, drowning them in desires. Olivia needed and wanted him. And he, too, wanted and needed her as much.

"Won't you lie down with me, please," she asked him. He got into bed with her. His arms provided comfort to the woman he cared for most, and feeling the warmth of her evoked his love. She clung to him as his fingers ran along the soft curves of her back while telling her how much he had missed her, telling her he was thankful for her safe return after a frightening experience. And telling her she was the center of everything pure and perfect in his life.

She answered his testimony of love, gently wrapping herself around him. Together then, they slipped into a sensual abyss of the tender rhythmic rise and fall of cotton sheets that covered them.

Some weeks later, the interstellar substation launched from Houston without fanfare. Media coverage was minimal. The mission, from its conception until its release into space was kept on a low profile. NASA also managed to keep connections between the Russian-conspired airport siege and the substation's activities out of the spotlight. For witness safety, news stories reported nothing about Professor Reece, who was the target of the miscreant perpetrators and intentionally kept investigations into the incident from public scrutiny. Fortunately, initial evidence suggested the corrupt assailants had acted alone and would face severe prosecution for their ambition, but consequently ill-fated takeover The sensationalized event soon faded to other political frenzies and human-interest stories dominating the media.

Chapter 19
Healing

On Tuesday, in late Fall, a rare and long-awaited rainfall poured over San Honesto for nearly five hours. The valley welcomed a reprieve from the prolonged arid conditions. By now, though, Olivia was back to teaching at UST, and the gentle afternoon shower persuaded her to drop by Eric's place before going home. She was still uncomfortable being alone after the terrifying airport attack. And the erratic nocturnal pattern, after being in Europe for so long, didn't allow sleep to come easily. Fortunately, being with Eric made her feel less vulnerable.

At home, Eric was on the computer paying bills. He was happy to see her when she hugged him from behind and blew a lustful "hello" into his ear.

"You look lovely today," he told her, admiring the tailored blazer and a tight-fitting black skirt that hugged her perfectly round hips. The black pumps added three inches to her graceful, five-feet-six balletic frame. In his opinion, there was something appealing about the appearance of intelligence and confidence: two assets she wore well. He suggested she take a short nap while he prepared a light dinner for them.

"How about a salad with plenty of cucumbers and tomatoes? What do you say?" His pampering made her happy.

"That's perfect. Thank you, Baby."

Their deepened affection for each other was a palpable reality. Their love and genuine trust bonded them. After dinner, Olivia was persuaded to stay the night. With him, she rested peacefully with Eric holding her until morning.

The next day, Lillie poured herself another vodka and tonic. She had become good at hiding a sad, melancholy life from those who knew her well. On the surface, she seemed to be just fine, but on the opposite side of the facade was something everyone failed to see. In reality, she was dealing with the debilitating effects of alcoholism, and she knew her drinking problem was gripping her. She could not get away from it as much as she desperately wanted to be free.

A part of her struggle was the result of transient and counterfeit happiness from liquor consumed daily. The other side of it was that Edward seemed to be clueless about Lillie's desperation to arbitrate their damaged marriage. She, too, wanted to repair what was broken in them, but they couldn't find a way beyond the impasse.

"What would you like to have with your steak tonight, Eddie?" Lillie asked her husband of thirty-eight years.

"Whatever you want. I'm not that hungry." His emotionless response was glacial.

Lillie was searching for a way to reach Edward and believed sharing more time together would help. In the past, counseling had not worked. She would be the first to admit that she'd intentionally ignored Edward's earlier efforts to get beyond the affair that became a wrecking ball onto a good marriage. Yet, the slightest possibility that his indiscretions might happen again constantly troubled her. She couldn't escape being locked in reminders of their damaged past.

"Any ideas about our next trip?" She asked, hoping to tap his interest in talking to her about anything at all.

"None." His comeback was unkind. He clicked through channels on the TV, showing little interest in hearing her solicitous words.

"Alright. Maybe I'll check on some safe places here in California since we're not traveling abroad for now, especially after what happened to Olivia. Let's say, we can go back East to see Brad and Grace in Boston or visit Vermont this time. How about that?"

Edward was annoyed by the wave of questions from Lillie and fixed his stare on the television. He'd become edgy, having no desire for small talk with her.

"Whatever you want to do, Lillie," he snapped back. He never looked in her direction. By choice, he stared blankly at a TV ad touting the incredible features of a kitchen gadget priced at nineteen-ninety-nine.

Lillie passed Edward a wary look and shook her head. She wondered if she'd made the right choice thirty-eight years ago. She wondered if she should have married him...or conceivably gone in a different direction with her life. But seeing him more dignified and handsome than ever, even in that uncomfortable exchange, Lillie knew she had made the right choice in life. Despite their past troubles, she loved him without condition. She went back to the kitchen, suppressing hurt from his attitude toward her and wishing for answers. She had maintained loyalty to him before and since his affair, and after searching her heart, had not found any reasons for Edward to cheat again. Even now, she could not find peace in their troubled times, - not even from a dirty martini left waiting for her on the kitchen counter. She took one more taste of vodka. The ringing of a rarely used landline phone startled her. Turning aside painful feelings, she answered the call from her daughter, glad to put off any thoughts of the rocky marriage.

"Hi, Darling."

"Hi, Mom. Eric and I will go to Charlotte this Friday to visit his mom and dad."

"Won't this be your first time meeting the Blakes in person?" She parted her lips for the last drops of the martini.

"Yes. After the scary airport thing, I'm nervous about flying. But I feel a little bit safer with Eric with me."

"You'll be alright. He will be there."

"By the way, Charlotte is a direct flight."

"Good. No point in changing planes." Lillie said.

"Yes, that's true."

"So, are you two getting more serious?"

"Mom! Please don't start that again." Olivia's stern, reaction caused her mother to recede.

"I'm sorry. I didn't mean to pry."

"It's okay." Olivia's tone softened. "I know you didn't mean to." She went on to explain. "We are not there yet in that marriage thing, and who knows, we may never get there, Mom. We have pretty good lives together right now without messing it up, and by making things...what are the words, too complicated? I'm just glad to finally meet his parents."

"But think of how much stronger you'd be together.

Couples who care for each other need that kind of bond."

Lillie considered her situation and the strong dissension she'd experienced with Edward minutes before Olivia called. Her heart was saddened. Even so, the conversation she'd promised herself to have with Olivia had yet to happen.

"I don't know much about marriage, Mom, except for what I've seen between you and Dad."

Olivia's reference to her parent's marriage caused Lillie to be reserved with advice about love, especially having just felt the pain of Edward's iciness. She wondered how she and Edward had been drifting apart for so long. Daily arguments outnumbered their friendly conversations. The painful differences and distance dividing them seemed too vast and stubbornly difficult to mend.

"Perhaps that is exactly why you should take your time, Sweetheart," Lillie finally said.

Ironically, it was a rare moment of shedding light on what would later be prophetic.

Three weeks later, on a Tuesday afternoon, Eric talked Olivia into staying overnight for a quiet dinner and a much-needed back rub. The pleasure of being with him relaxed her, and they turned in early, planning to walk the lake at daybreak.

Around 3:00 A.M the following morning, Olivia's phone vibrated on the nightstand. When she didn't awaken, Eric answered. He immediately knew something was wrong by the caller's frantic voice.

"Hello," said Eric, digging his fingers into sleepy eyes.

"Eric, this is Edward Reece. I need to speak to my daughter."

"Yes, Sir, Mr. Reece. Let me get her for you." He lightly tapped his bedmate until she stirred. "Olivia, wake up, Baby."

"What? What's going on?"

"Your dad wants to speak with you. Here you are."

"Dad? What's wrong?" Sleepiness turned into panic.

Eric anxiously watched as her face changed from fear to horror. She sprang up in bed, pulling the sheet beneath her chin. Edward spoke quickly, hoping to minimize his daughter's worries. He knew she would want to rush home, and driving too fast would be unsafe at that hour.

"Your mother is at Memorial Hospital in the ICU," Edward explained the crisis. Before he finished speaking, Olivia was delirious. "Calm down, Honey. There is nothing you can do up here if you get all upset. Please, I need you to be levelheaded as this unfolds," her father pleaded.

"Oh my God!"

Meanwhile, Eric heard the fear in her voice while returning from the kitchen. He sprinted back to the bedroom. She insisted, "What happened? Tell me, Dad!"

Olivia felt as if she was suffocating. Edward nervously explained that Lillie had suffered a stroke with complications and was taken to intensive care an hour earlier. He went on to say she was not out of danger and doctors had performed some initial procedures to minimize the severity of the outcome, provided she recovered at all.

"Dad, no! I am on my way. I can come right now."

"Let me talk to Eric." Eric's protective arms were calming. Without looking up at him and burying her face in his bare chest, she weakly passed him the phone, nearly dropping it.

"Yes, Sir, Mr. Reece. Whatever I need to do," Eric unconsciously nodded. "Yes, Sir. Yes. Bye."

Olivia jumped out of bed and a wave of bed linens followed her, hitting the floor in a rumpled pile. Eric watched helplessly, unsure what should have been done to relieve her. He didn't have an answer. He knew there weren't enough consoling words for her and believed being near her was the best thing to give. By now, she was hurrying to get dressed, darting about like an agitated animal in a caged room. Her only thought was getting to Santa Cruz right away.

"Gotta' go up there now," Olivia announced, grabbing the gray pinstriped business dress tossed across the nearby chair. She wiggled it on over the silk, royal blue lingerie that he liked on her.

"Hey, wait a second. Let me tell you what your dad wants you to do." His tired eyes were pleading with her.

Frantically half listening to the man trying to set her fears at rest, she harshly demanded, "What!"

"Your dad wants you to wait until daylight to go up there. He said there is no need for you to come right now because the doctors have done all they can do to stabilize your mom's condition. They're going to follow up with more tests as soon as the labs open later in the morning."

"Eric, you know me!" She blasted back at him

before realizing the sharpness of her tone. "There is no way I am going to sit here when my mother is in a hospital bed, maybe hanging on to a thin string of life, and not go to her!"

He stared at her but said nothing.

She reacted. "I cannot do that, Eric!"

For the first time, she was feeling the fear of losing control of a situation. In times before, she'd dealt with many unsettling crises but handled them by facing the dragons of her fears. This time, though, she couldn't control what was happening. And she didn't like the way it felt.

"Olivia, listen. Please." He walked over and gave her a tissue as the flow of tears trickled onto his bare chest.

"Your father has it under control for now. Thank God this didn't happen when you were in England."

"Yes." A muffled response rose from her between sniffles and more tears; he was thankful to be there to hold her.

"What I want you to do for me is to be clear-headed enough to take care of whatever has to be done before we drive up to Santa Cruz at sunrise."

But as he tried to ease her fears, he knew she was inconsolable. Her tearful eyes foretold her anguish.

"You're going up there with me?" She frowned, appearing puzzled.

"Tell me, Olivia, why wouldn't I?"

His solemn promise mollified her. She backed onto the bed, sitting motionless with hands that turned to clenched fists. For a time, in the bedroom, she stared at the clock on the nightstand that blinked 5:00 A.M. in bright red.

She would insist on leaving as soon as the sun came up. Before leaving for Santa Cruz, Olivia reached out to UST, including contacting Ms. Marshall and the Dean.

A talk with Lillie weeks before came to mind. It was when Lillie longingly talked about matrimony and the strength of being together as a couple, and tellingly, she'd spoken of what it could mean in situations like this one. It was suddenly clear what her mother had meant.

On reflection, while searching for missed signals, she wondered what her mother might have been dealing with when she shared her opinions about love and relationships during their talks. Or, for that matter, what kind of torment had triggered the severe condition Lillie was now facing?

The day before Lillie had the stroke, she was busy volunteering as usual. Predictably, she had started her day at the crack of dawn. Her first stop was at the elementary school several blocks from her house. By 8:30 A.M., she'd donated two hundred boxes of crayons, coloring books, and a one-thousand-dollar check from the Reece family, with the same gift promised for the following year.

Later in the day, after one last stop to help bag groceries at a neighborhood food bank, Lillie was ready to go home. She was fighting a splitting headache that would not cease, and taking a pain reliever some hours earlier had not helped to ease her discomfort. The frustrating drive home in heavy traffic exacerbated the nagging pounding in her head.

Cars with impatient drivers in every lane on the highway worsened the attack on Lillie's growing tension. Vehicles moved along at less than five miles per hour, and the congested roadway didn't get her home any faster. Her head was exploding nonstop throughout the winding vehicular crawl.

Once home, Lillie planned to shower and nap before preparing dinner. When she got there, Lillie found Edward leisurely stretched across the sofa and mindlessly watching TV. His behavior was disappointing since he'd offered to cut vegetables for homemade soup and had not done so.

She didn't argue with him, although his behavior caused her appetite to disappear. Because of that, she went straight to bed with plans of eating a good breakfast the next day.

Around midnight, Lillie was awake. Sleep was elusive, so she got up for a drink of water since her headache was pounding away. She was overcome with persistent pain and feeling dazed. All of a sudden, everything around her went black. She collapsed to the floor.

Minutes later, Edward would call out to her, and when she didn't answer, he discovered her slumped in a corner of the kitchen floor. Knocked out from hitting her head during the fall, her breathing was shallow. Edward was suddenly slammed into a tailspin, and it felt like a sudden punch in the middle of his gut. He dialed 911. The emergency service immediately dispatched an ambulance and tried to calm him as they rushed to his address. Confused and impetuous, Edward hung up on the dispatcher and redialed the number. This time, the emergency workers persuaded him not to hang up and talked with him until the ambulance arrived. The EMTs took Lillie to the downtown medical center, and from there, Edward called Olivia.

Right at dawn, the anxious couple left for Santa Cruz. The long drive was shadowed by concerns of what might happen to Lillie. Olivia nervously stared ahead in traffic and tried to set aside images of her mother lying on a hospital bed. Sensing her nervousness, Eric caringly glanced at her, recognizing that no shred of comfort would be found in Olivia until she saw her mother.

"It's going to be alright." He said to her. "We will be there soon. Let's keep praying hard for the best outcome." He clutched her trembling hand.

"Thanks." Her lip quivered as she turned in his direction.

"I'm scared, Eric. I don't know how to handle what's happening."

"I know that, Olivia. You don't have to worry. I am here." He was doing his best to calm her. She had stayed awake after the pre-dawn phone call from Edward, unable to rest before leaving for the hospital. Halfway to Santa Cruz, she finally fell asleep, with Eric pushing above the speed limit to get there.

Within two nerve-racking hours, they reached the hospital. Edward Reece looked like a man lost in oblivion. He was exhausted. His wrinkled shirttail was untucked, without regard for fashion rules. As one might expect, the older man's jumbled appearance was the result of being out of bed for nearly fourteen hours. The prickly gray and unshaven shadow confirmed the events leading to where he was at the time. Edward stopped his nervous pacing when the couple reached him in the ICU waiting room.

"Dad!" Olivia rushed to him. To her, he clung tightly and quietly sobbed. "I couldn't help her. I didn't know what to do, Olivia. I was scared."

"Come now, Dad. You did just what you should have done."

Edward was grief-stricken and blind to his daughter's attempts to calm him. He stared down at his tight-fisted hands. "Then why is she here, Baby? Why!"

"Not something you had any control over, Dad. None of us could have predicted this."

"No. I know I could've done more," Olivia's father stammered. "I should have! They took too damned long to get to her! I kept calling the ambulance and I kept waiting. I had to wait for them too damn long, Olivia!" His anxiety caused a flush of red to invade his watering eyes.

"I'm sure the ambulance got there in ample time. It's okay." Helplessly, she tried comforting him.

Her dad looked toward Eric, "Son, thank you for getting here quick with my daughter. I don't know if she would've made it here without you. I'm in your debt."

Eric nodded iappreciation. Edward Reece's words were kind, but he would have been there with them regardless.

"Where is the doctor?" Olivia begged Edward. Her dad's weariness, compounded with exhaustion, blurred his thinking. His tired shoulders slumped. Olivia's eyes met Eric's; she was uncertain, too. He motioned for her to sit down.

The doctor, whose stark white, unkempt hair suggested long hours on duty, entered the waiting room a short time later. His manner was bleak. The waiting trio rushed him all at once.

"Mr. Reece, as we discussed earlier, the prognosis is uncertain at this juncture." Edward suspected the doctor's report was cautiously doubtful. And by then, his emotions were getting the best of him.

His tall frame towered over the doctor. "What!" He exclaimed. "You have to tell me more than this, Doctor Lind!" His hands shot up as he questioned the lack of sufficient information. "Listen, explain Lillie's condition to us right now!"

In one shot, his daughter positioned herself squarely in front of the doctor with questions of her own. Her focus was set on him. The doctor, taken by an unexpected intrusion into the confidential conversation, frowned cautiously at the unfamiliar woman.

"I'm Dr. Lind, Chief Neurologist. We haven't met." Thrown off guard by her aggression, he turned to Edward Reece for permission to continue.

Edward obligingly introduced his daughter and Eric to the doctor, noting that Olivia would have authority as his wife's proxy in his absence. He then pressured Dr. Lind to continue with his vague prognosis.

"Well, Sir, the results are not back yet. But it appears Mrs. Reece suffered a massive embolic stroke, which is when a blood clot forms in another part of the body and moves to the brain. Hemiparesis may have occurred."

"Oh, my goodness. " Edward cried out. Clearly he was overwrought with fear.

She interrupted the doctor, "What about therapy? What about surgery? Can either one of them help her?"

"It is tough to say right now and too soon to tell. But we are going to do our best. Again, the lab results will give us more information with in-depth results later."

"Let me get this straight. You don't have any updated information about my mother's condition?"

The doctor removed his eyeglasses, as if looking for answers in the oversized bifocal frame, he searched the small waiting room for insight, and shook his head.

Eric hugged Olivia and watched her reaction as Dr. Lind dispensed the troubling news. When the doctor left, Olivia combed her mind for answers to the crisis. First, she thought of William Gibson's wife, Emily, the nurse. She immediately put a call through to William, nervously waiting until he answered.

"Hi Olivia, I heard the news. How is your mom doing?"

"William, I guess she's doing okay right now. I appreciate your thoughts. I know Emily is very busy at San Honesto Medical, but would you please have her call me whenever she has a free minute? I want to understand my mom's condition better, and I trust Emily."

"Sure, I'll do that."

"I need your help with this, William, please."

"Of course, Olivia. She has left for work and is the Head Nurse on her shift today. But I'll let her know as soon as I hang up."

"Thanks. Doing that for me means a lot."

Edward, Olivia, and Eric remained at the hospital for

hours, waiting for updates on Lillie's condition, only to get scanty details. Later, while they waited, Dr. Lind promised to provide a full report as soon as the lab results were reviewed. "This could take some time today," he explained.

The trio left the hospital after hours of agonizingly empty waiting. Going home, Edward sat on the back seat of Eric's car nervously recalling what happened to Lillie. During the short drive, anxiousness and worry invaded the silence.

Edward's distraught eyes roamed the Santa Cruz streets while thinking of what happened to Lillie. He was feeling helpless and fearful of his wife's horrifying condition.

At the house, Olivia prepared a light dinner for them, of which little was eaten, and afterward, Edward went to bed promptly. He offered a heartfelt 'thank you' to the couple before turning in to rest.

That night, the sobering effects of Lillie's emergency prompted the couple to talk about the future. Eric promised whatever she needed.

"I am so afraid, Eric. And I don't have a solution to this... As I look back, the airport attack was less frightening for me. Babe, I don't know..." Her words dropped off and she was unable to finish them.

Everything happening to her was knotted with anxiety. She found it hard to verbalize her feelings.

"This situation is unknown." She went on. "It's a sober reminder that there is an 'inevitable end' to our existence as we know it."

"Baby, no one ever plans for something like this to happen."

"I know." She interrupted, "But this situation has too many moving parts, and I can't get control of them."

"You have me. I'm not going anywhere. I promise you that."

They held each other in her childhood bedroom filled with her high school memories, but the worrisome thoughts of Lillie's circumstance continued.

Early the next morning. Eric's phone buzzed in his jacket pocket from across the room. He moved Olivia's arm from his chest to answer the call before the last ring. She was sound asleep.

"Good morning," Eric answered.

"Hey, Man, I got your message. How's your lady doing, " asked Patrick.

It was the same buddy who arranged for Eric to rent the Piper Turbo that was used to fly Olivia in Kenmore before Christmas.

"She's okay. Not sure about the status of her mom, though. I appreciate the call from you, Patrick."

Eric's eyes laid upon Olivia, and he noticed that she was sleeping contently. His heart ached for her because he knew she was worried about her mother's medical crisis.

Right after talking to Patrick, a call from Brinks came in with promises to keep things under control at Velocity. As he ended the second call, he accidentally dropped his FOB on the floor, which caused her to stir. Her sleepy eyes were pleased to see him close by. She slept for thirty more minutes and finally got out of bed.

"Morning."

"Hey," she greeted him. He studied her face to see how she was doing.

"Sweetheart, your dad has already gone to the hospital. He didn't want to disturb you and left a note for us to come down there later."

She plunged into action, scrambling from the room to get her shoes and purse stashed near the garage door. She'd slept fully dressed in case of an urgent call from the hospital. There would be nothing to stop her from getting back there quickly.

"Hold on. It would be best if you got something to eat before you go down there. Remember, you barely ate your dinner last night. You should eat something."

She blew off the suggestion of eating. Food didn't interest Olivia, and she needed to be at her mother's bedside.

"I'm good for now. I'll get something later."

Eric walked across the room where she'd begun staging an exit. He kissed her forehead and wrapped his arm around her and said, "Come with me."

Though reluctant, Olivia conceded to his bidding out of exhaustion or anxiousness. It was unclear which of the two conditions persuaded her. Nevertheless, she yielded to his encouragement.

He guided her to the kitchen, where he'd found cereal, fresh fruit, and chilled orange juice taken from the fridge. In his judgment, it was vital for her to get nourishment before returning to the uncontrolled, rapidly developing crisis. He knew he had to take care of her. At a place he'd already prepared for Olivia, he said, "Sit down, Honey. You need to eat. I need you to eat. I need you to have all your strength for your mom, your dad, and me."

He helped her into the chair and poured milk on a small mound of wheat squares in a bowl. She fumbled with the spoon and eventually started to eat, mindlessly chewing the dry, tasteless cereal. The grass-like cubes scratched her throat.

After a few coarse bites were swallowed, she remarked, "I want you to know how much you mean to me and how much joy you've added to my life, Eric." The circumstances of Lillie's critical state urged the confession.

He promised, "You don't have to say anything else. We will make it through this."

"You're right," she responded while sipping orange juice. She chewed more cereal as she thought of what the day would bring.

While feeling grateful for breakfast, Olivia admired her childhood backyard. Lillie's summer garden showed signs of a forthcoming change. Flowers had wilted, and the colorful hues had faded to shades of gold and brown. Lillie's wind chimes tinkled as a sudden breeze fanned across the back porch where partygoers had socialized one Christmas ago. It was also the same place where prayers went up for Olivia on her way to Europe. Now, it was Olivia's turn to pray for her mother. And she had to pray as hard as she could.

At the hospital, Edward's gloomy mindset left no questions about the extent of his torment. For him, the crisis was difficult to explain. He didn't know what to do and didn't know what might happen to Lillie. He was relegated to the bewilderment of waiting. Above all else, patience was what he had to endure. In Edward's heart, patience, though it was a challenge, had to win.

When the couple made it to the hospital, it was close to 11:30 A.M. There, in the third private ICU room, was Lillie, with nurses and technicians hovering and probing over what seemed to be every inch of her. The monitors made puffing, binging, and wheezing sounds that drowned out the quiet conversations among the staff. A nurse came in to check Lillie's vital signs and glanced hopefully toward Edward. To him, everything was dreamlike. He sat there braced by his worries, squeezing his wife's hand and fixing his eyes on her ashen, motionless face. Time and again, he leaned over the metal bed rail to kiss her chapped lips. He was troubled and afraid to leave Lillie's side.

"Dad, you need a break," his daughter said when she entered the room.

"I'm okay, Baby."

"Please, Dad. We will be here with Mom. Go!"

"Can't do it. I need to be here."

"Okay," she finally said. She didn't want to further upset Edward. They sat in a silent vigil for hours.

By the end of the second day, Olivia persuaded Eric to return to San Honesto.

"There is no way I'm gonna' let you jeopardize the contracts your team's been working on."

"Olivia, I need to be with you and your Dad."

"You've been so wonderful to be here with me. The university has approved for me to be away for a while.

The dean is aware of what's happening and I'm returning by next Friday. My graduate students will pitch in to help with my classes."

"Okay," Eric responded. He was cautiously wondering if Olivia and Edward would be alright. This situation was new territory for all of them.

She continued to convince him. "Don't worry; my grad assistants will get real-time teaching experience. I won't be there to scrutinize them." She wanted Eric to know that everything was under control.

"Yeah, yeah, yeah," he let out a long sigh, kissing her and heading for the door to leave, but with apparent second thoughts, he turned around.

"Are you sure you're fine?"

"Yes, Go! Eric, we will be alright." She walked over and put her arms tightly around him once again.

His tender embrace foretold his love. "I will call you the minute I get home," he said.

As soon as Eric reached San Honesto, a call came in from Allen Brinks. He needed to update his boss. The first bit of information was that Lukas from Ergowilst wanted to speak with him immediately.

"He complained that he tried calling you several times, and you didn't call him back."

"What the hell, Allen. I was with Olivia. Didn't you tell him that?"

"I did, Man," Allen answered. "He didn't seem to be

concerned about that. He said he had some urgent information on Klaus Industrial and the Barcelona trip, and said you needed to know."

"Lukas doesn't own me. I'll call him when I am damned ready."

"Right, Man."

Hours into the evening, back home, Lukas called Eric again.

"Hey, Eric, is there any way we can get Olivia to talk to Hans Schweinsteiger tomorrow? He will be here in the U.S. Do you think she'd join in a conference call with us?"

"What about?"

"Her Krausberg work."

"Seriously, Lukas? Her mom is in the hospital. You know how protective Olivia has been about her research. Even with me. I would NEVER, EVER ask her to do that. Above that, it would be a breach of my trust. I know you guys know about the work she's been doing, but damn, Man, there's no way she was going to help Klaus, who was denied a chance to be a part of the substation project. Sorry, Bro. I'm not the one. Why didn't you tell me that Hans was the same guy who was supposed to meet with Olivia's group in Birmingham at the Carlyle Hotel? What's up with that, Man? And I assure you, Lukas, I'm gonna' tell her about Hans' request. What he's asking is not right. Definitely not right."

Lukas was put off by Eric's angry reaction. Since he was part of so many lucrative jobs at Ergowilst, he thought Eric would oblige what he wanted. That didn't happen. By then, the substation had already been put into orbit. It was having an enormously positive impact on enhancing international communication security since launched. So why were they still pursuing Olivia's work? Eric would eventually warn Olivia about the seemingly clandestine pursuit of the Krausberg Effect research, a significant part of the satellite design, of which she was constantly protective. It would later be revealed that Interpol was surveilling and investigating German scientist Hans Schweinsteiger, who was suspected of being involved in the airport attack. Dr. Stossburg, on the other hand, was not guilty of any wrongdoing, and his interest in collaborating with Olivia was genuine.

Meanwhile, Lillie's condition was sporadic. Months would pass before there were any convincing signs of significant recovery. Yet Edward remained at his wife's bedside. Over time, the hospital employees expected and welcomed Edward in Lillie's room, believing his presence helped her heal.

Grace and Brad Reece called from Boston daily to check on Lillie's progress, offering to travel to California if needed, but Edward declined their kindness. Doris, Edward's only sister, became a supportive anchor for them.

After weeks of treatment, Lillie was moved out of the ICU to a rehab facility where she received therapeutic care. Within a reasonable time period, she began responding to his constant presence. Each day she greeted him with "I love you, Eddie." And although it took a lot of effort for her to silently mouth the words, she didn't want the chance of reconciliation to slip by.

And Edward, visibly eager to see the signs of healing, would hold her hand practically all day, expressing the same to her. For the first time in many years, the couple was trying to repair their differences. There was no bitterness. Remnants of their last few troubled years disappeared in the awakening of the ear of losing each other.

As Lillie recovered, her family implored doctors to use all measures to help her heal. The neurologists were astounded by how well she was mending because they hadn't expected her to do so. During intense therapy for twelve weeks, she regained strength and cognitive capacity to communicate, although with limitations. Nothing could have pleased the Reece family more, especially Edward. For him, it was having a second lease on the love they'd found decades before. In many ways, the misfortune that overturned Lillie's life had also brought Olivia and Eric closer.

Chapter 20
Endearment

One afternoon, while driving back to San Honesto from an overnight visit with her parents, Olivia got an unexpected call from Eric. He was in New York to meet with prospective clients. He'd been promised multiple East Coast contracts by the company's CEO. The lucrative opportunity would substantially increase Velocity's annual earnings. But when he arrived at the New York office on the twenty-second floor, he discovered that Ergowilst had intervened and canceled the sit-down, claiming to have decided against recommending Velocity. Did Lukas cancel the meeting to get back at Eric for failing to come through for him with Olivia? Eric didn't know if this were true and, until now, hadn't given it any thought. However, he was disappointed with the unnecessary trip and quickly started devising a plan to return home.

His commercial pilot friend, Patrick, who recently started a commuter service for wealthy clientele, had purchased a four-seater Cessna from a German import dealer in Canada three weeks prior. The plane, which was temporarily stowed in New York, was designed and built by a German-based company.

Eric knew Patrick wanted to bring the aircraft to the West Coast but was bogged down with international flights, making it impossible to get the aircraft home. Knowing his friend's dilemma, Eris phoned Patrick and offered to fly the Cessna West. Patrick welcomed the idea right away. To Eric's advantage, flying the Cessna to California would be a better option than a commercial flight. Photos of the new Cessna revealed a magnificent machine he was eager to fly.

He immediately called Olivia to let her know his plans for leaving New York. His feelings poured out to Olivia. "I want to be home, Olivia. I'm missing you like nobody's business today."

"How long will the flight take, Eric? Don't you need to rest?" She wanted answers.

"I'm not sure how long it'll take, but Patrick guessed it could be a six-hour trip, broken into two segments if I refueled between here and California. It won't be as fast as a commercial flight, but I won't be stuck here in New York either."

"Where will you refuel?" She asked while turning her car off the exit onto Petaluma Avenue toward the condo.

"The flight plan has me stopping in Oklahoma City."
"This is a solo flight for you, and that concerns me."
"I will be alright. Gotta get back home soon."
Not wanting to continue his talk about flying alone,

he interjected, "I will let you know the flight details as soon as I can secure the plane from Kennedy Airport. Patrick said I could be airborne in a couple of hours."

"Oh. Okay." She tried hard not to show concern, but the thought of him flying alone in an unfamiliar plane at night troubled her.

Patrick had helped him obtain the necessary flight hours to earn a license in a short span. There was no question of Eric's cockpit readiness. Patrick trusted him wholeheartedly. However, even with so many hours of flight time, the extended solo journey would still be new territory for Eric.

On the way to get the Cessna from the hangar, he called Olivia. The inferior Bluetooth system in the rental car was bothersome, so he disengaged the connection and talked directly into his phone as he drove toward Kennedy Airport.

"Hey, Babe."

"I've been waiting for you to call me back." By then, she had arrived at her place in San Honesto, checked the landline voicemail, and unpacked her overnight bag.

"Yeah. Sorry that it's taken this long." He apologized.

She exhaled quietly, trying hard to shield her worries. Knowing that Eric was flying the unfamiliar plane was disconcerting to her. Something in her wouldn't let that feeling go.

"You and I can own a plane one day," he said. He appeared to be unconcerned about the flight back home. And though Olivia could not control the worry, in many ways, her caution was probably unwarranted. In her heart, she knew he was a capable pilot, and she believed in him. Her concerns momentarily quieted when he said something else.

"Olivia, these long cross-country flights give a man a lot of time to think of and appreciate his blessings." His words began in the third person as if it made saying them easier, but then he said, "And for me, you've become the most important blessing of all."

"Thank you," she responded.

She closed her eyes, replayed his words, and said. "I'm feeling the same way you're feeling, Eric."

"Do you?" He questioned her.

"I do," said she. "I have for a long time now. It's just that sometimes I'm too hesitant to say."

He persisted, "Why is that true, Olivia?" He wanted her to know he was listening intently to what she shared with him.

"Oh, I don't know. It's just well..." She paused, not saying anymore.

"Say whatever you're feeling, please."

"Someone once said that love is an overrated emotion. And for so long, I also believed it to be overrated. But with you, it's been different. It has been more than that."

He soberly listened to her unveiled feelings and nearly overshot the exit ramp that would take him to the airfield.

"Hold on. Let me catch this turn." He switched lanes, narrowly missing a car that was attempting to take the same exit.

"I'm just about at the hangar. Let me call you right back after I drop this rental off. Give me fifteen to get to the airstrip."

❦

He enabled the navigation system to take him to Conduit Avenue and then to Federal Circle, where he returned the borrowed car. He took a JFK Expressway shuttle to the nearby hangars. Once there, he called Olivia. She answered immediately.

"Will it be okay to see you tonight or first thing tomorrow? What time are you going to campus? I've been wanting to tell you about what I overheard in Barcelona. Plus, there is something else I want to ask you."

"You know you can see me anytime you want."

"Yeah. I've been thinking of my talk with Mom at Christmas, and the one I had with her when you were in England, about how I should be keeping the bloodline going," his words came amid a subtle chuckle.

"Yes, I remember." She had become curious about what he was telling her since he appeared to be wrestling with his thoughts. His words trailed off.

The sound of his brisk steps making it across the asphalt echoed in the background. She could barely hear him, and something about 'forever' was heard, but the other words weren't clear.

"What time will you be home tonight?" She held back the longing to keep the conversation going. It was more important that he remained focused on the upcoming flight.

"I should be in L.A. at ten-thirty. Don't forget, I will fuel up again halfway, about three hours into the flight. I know the plane can make the distance without stopping, but I feel better about making the stop as a safety checkpoint."

"Alright, will you call me or send a text to let me know you've made it that far? Once back here, call me, and I'll come for you."

"I promise to call you."

He was eager to leave New York City. He double checked his leather duffel bag, which had become a constant companion on cross-country treks. He'd carefully tucked away a tiny black box inside the zippered lining.

"I hope it's the right size," he excitedly thought. The velvet box contained a two-carat engagement ring. He'd begun putting money away and luckily ran across the five-thousand-dollar solitaire in an Upper Manhattan jewelry store. He happened upon the exclusive jeweler as he was about to leave the city for the airstrip. It was as if the ring had been waiting there for him. The serendipitous discovery cemented his plans to propose to her.

He would ask her as soon as he was back in California. Given his past with Jasmine, he was hopeful about Olivia's reaction to his proposal. All he knew then was that he wanted her to be his wife.

While waiting for the aviation paperwork to be cleared, his memory fell upon his last time at home in Charlotte.

On Christmas Eve, Eric had opened up to his mother about the woman who unwittingly captured his heart in the San Honesto shopping plaza. The memory of that night and the conversation with his mother was telling.

"When your Dad and I met Olivia not long ago, we knew exactly why you care for her the way you do."

On that Christmas night, his mother sat near the fireplace wrapping the last of several gifts.

"Yes. Olivia is special." Eric had revealed

Her image popped into his head as he stretched out on the couch with hands clasped behind his head. His mind scrolled through memories of her.

"I'm glad you've met a woman who appreciates you and shares your dreams, Son."

His father, a man of few words, listened in and agreed with his wife, pointing out that the key to enduring relationships starts with genuine trust. The elder Mr. Blake then put more logs on the fire.

Although his mother readily praised her son's new love, she'd also never spoken harshly of his previous mates. Beyond wanting grandchildren, she rarely offered opinions about Eric's relationships. It was not her business to meddle in his personal life, though she'd mistakenly crossed that line once in a while, as most mothers occasionally would.

"I got lucky this time. I think I'm really lucky."

"Yes, Son, you are," she confirmed in a quiet manner.

"Before her, I was beginning to believe I wouldn't find real love. I was about to give up. She is such an amazing woman, Mom," he declared on Christmas Eve. He couldn't remember if he'd ever described Jasmine to his mother with the same joy.

"I've known you all of your life, Son." She smiled at him with love. "But blessings happen just when they are supposed to, and your meeting Olivia was a blessing. She is a loving and caring partner for you, Eric."

Satisfied to have shared his feelings, he got up from the couch, sweetly kissed his mother, and handed her a gift decorated with a large red bow. "Merry Christmas, Mom. I love you."

Now, several months after that Christmas Eve night in Charlotte with his mother, Eric wanted to end Olivia's doubts about his safety in flying alone, as well as any doubts about his love for her. He hurried to the Cessna in hangar fourteen for the solo trip from New York. He was anxious to take off. "Just letting you know I'm about to leave New York."

"I was getting antsy. I thought you would've left before now."

"No. Not yet. There was someone ahead of me. I called Patrick to give him the flight plan. He told me this plane has a superb navigational system and is very easy to handle, even though he has flown the plane only once. He is happy with this European model that was built in Germany."

"I guess that's great." She let out an uneasy laugh, not understanding all of the aircraft jargon.

"Yeah. By the way, I should get home at 10:30 P.M. It occurs to me that is way past your bedtime." His humored comment intended to keep her from fretting over the long flight.

"I don't care what time it is; please let me know you're back home safe."

"Madame, what's my reward for reporting to you when I return?" he playfully insisted.

"Don't try to bribe me, Eric Blake," she answered him sternly. "Just come back to me tonight, please."

"Alright then. I'm gonna' fly this thing back like I'm on an Air Force fighter. Listen, Pretty Woman, you'd better be ready for me."

"Whatever. Eric, I love you... need you... and want you here with me. Please come home safe."

He was excited. He kept thinking about what he might say or do when he declared his love and offered the ring to her in less than twenty-four hours. He just had to figure out the best place to do it. It ought to be memorable. So, he thought of every possible scenario, including a drive back to the Moon Eclipse in Long Beach, rolling on the edge of the Pacific Ocean, and stopping somewhere along the way. Would he ask her as soon as he was home? He wasn't sure of what to do, but the flight to L.A. would give him plenty of time to think about it.

Airport officials completed his readiness to fly. "Okay, Mr. Blake, you're all set. You will be taxiing out of runway four. We've cleared your documents, and you're good to go," confirmed the man sitting at the front desk in the private aircraft facility.

Eric went to the hangar where Voyager, Patrick's prized Cessna, was prepared for departure. He'd soon be airborne.

Quickly walking toward the aircraft, he saw the nose of the plane poking out of the fifty-foot storage area. On either side, in identical spaces, were two other planes stored by their wealthy owners.

"Someday." He fantasized as he admired the sleek contours of Voyager, sliding his hand along the body of the superbly unsullied machine. It had a range of 3,000 nautical miles. The dominant color was pure white, but the prominent black and red stripes on either side made this impeccably crafted plane stand out against others in the hangar. The aircraft was breathtaking to someone who loved flying as much as he did. It was one of many small planes designed and built by Klaus Industrial in Hamburg, Germany, that could fly well over 500 knots.

In the cockpit, he contemplated having Olivia beside him on the flight. She would have marveled at mountains that revealed an incredible nighttime backdrop and a skyline enveloped in the darkness of night, jeweled with the brightest stars. She would like that.

She frequently talked about more outdoor road trips, and Eric excitedly welcomed her willingness to try new things with him. He thought, though, of her as a refined woman, accustomed to nice things, and roughing it on the road with her would be a fun-loving adventure, doing things like cooking fish on a lakeside. It would be pleasantly amusing to see her in that kind of setting. But what he loved most about her was a willingness to accept him just as much as he respected everything about her.

More times than he could remember, she'd told him that his self-assuredness was endearing to her. Those words from her made him feel powerful and loved. He, too, desired to please her and didn't care about the sacrifice or expense.

He was ready to leave New York City because San Honesto was nothing like the Big Apple, with millions of people. As a result, the canceled meeting was not a disappointment. Plus, not having access to Patrick's plane would have meant an unnecessary overnight stay in a pricey hotel.

Now settled in the cockpit, he mentally played the flight checklist to guide the phases of being airborne from takeoff to landing. He summarized the flight sequence and confirmed his route. In preparation for departure, he reviewed the flight route and the reported forecasts along the flight path. The conditions for flying would be good, as far as he could tell.

His eyes traced the horizon after silently meditating in prayer. It was the ritual he practiced on every flight. Anxious to get started, Eric taxied to the runway. More excited now about going home, he revved the engine and steered the plane down the slick, black tarmac, increasing the speed for a smooth liftoff. He anxiously pulled back on the throttle and ascended several thousand feet into the dark, nighttime clouds. He was airborne. His plan? To reach a maximum cruising altitude of twenty thousand feet and to push a speed of one-hundred-sixty knots toward home.

1:32 A.M. The landline phone rattled her. It was discomforting to hear the silence broken at such an early hour after her mother's life-changing incident. The ringing phone jolted Olivia out of slumber as she waited during the night on the couch, all the while drifting in and out of sleep. She planned to be awake whenever Eric called.

Many hours before, he should have landed in Los Angeles. Surprisingly, though, he didn't call from Oklahoma City as promised. She thought of myriad reasons for not hearing from him and intended to get all over his case for not keeping his word.

She was puzzled. "Why didn't he call me before now? And I wonder why he's calling on this line," she mumbled, barely awake and rushing across the room to answer before it stopped ringing.

"Hey, Eric, where do you want me to pick you up?" She spoke quickly, ready to chide him for not calling her,

"Is this Olivia Reece?" A frantic, unfamiliar voice was on the call.

"Yes, it is. Who is this," she asked, pressing the phone to her ear. Static could be heard, causing noisy interference.

"It's Patrick, Eric's buddy."

"Patrick? Why in the world are you calling me at this hour?"

"Olivia, something's happened. I've been told Eric and the plane are missing."

"What! Please don't tell me that. I've been waiting all night for him to call me!"

"I don't have a lot of information for you now but I'm hoping to hear from authorities pretty soon."

The horrifying news from Patrick was dizzying, and she couldn't find the words to respond. "I am calling you, Olivia, because he gave your contact numbers to me weeks ago should something ever happen. They haven't found the plane. The search may take days or weeks, so let's prepare for that."

She was terrified and shaking uncontrollably.

She went through her head for an explanation. But she needed Patrick to tell her more. "No! No! Don't tell me that, Patrick, please don't! No!"

"Is there someone there with you right now?"

She ignored his question, now trying to control her racing pulse.

"Oh, God. What's happened to him? Patrick, they've got to find him!"

"I want you to call someone to tell them what's happened. You don't need to be alone right now. Is there anyone there? What about a friend?"

She was shuddering, near to the point of convulsions. Frightening images of what might have happened raced through her.

"Yes, I have someone. But how can I reach you?" She pressured him.

After giving her as much information as possible, he hung up. Olivia's heart was hammering out of control. She shakily clutched the gold locket, praying that Patrick's phone call was a nightmare from which she'd woken up. Now weakly coherent, she followed Patrick's advice to call someone but didn't want to upset her parents with the horrible news. Instead, Lora's phone number was dialed. Fifteen minutes later, Lora and Keith were there with her.

On the third morning, they found the plane. Lora called Olivia after hearing the breaking news. "Hey, I just heard."

Olivia questioned. "What's going on, Lora?"

Oh, you don't know?"

"No."

"I'm on my way to work now and the news is reporting they found the wreckage."

Olivia wanted to speak but couldn't. She was panicked and no words came from her as she waited for Lora to give more details.

"Are you there? I'm so sorry, Dear. I thought they would have called you before the media caught wind of it."

"No. I didn't know." Olivia's breathing was choppy, and hyperventilation made her balance unstable. Her back flattened against the kitchen wall to keep from falling.

"What did they say?"

"Not much, except they are doing an investigation on site by sending the Safety Board folks out there."

"Where?"She was shaking.

"I think they said somewhere in Arizona."

"This is awful, Lora. I don't know what to do."

"Stay calm, but call your parents with this news because you don't want this to upset them. It was hard enough on them when it first happened. Eric's family will likely call you today, too. You want to talk to someone you can trust. Someone who will be looking out for you."

"Yes, I hear you, Lora."

"You know how your mom cares for Eric. And she's doing better now. You wouldn't want to unsettle the progress she's made."

Olivia's emotions moved like a speeding roller coaster. She wanted to break down, but she couldn't afford to. Eric would have wanted her to put the brakes on her escalating fears despite the mortifying circumstances. She took Lora's advice and called her dad, who was at home caring for Lillie. Edward had become increasingly able to manage things as Lillie's health improved. In earlier weeks, Lillie had shown encouraging signs of gaining more independence. Though it was happening at a snail's pace, Her activities since returning home were far better. And the doctors' prognosis indicated there could be at least ninety-five percent recovery.

"Morning, Olivia."

"Good morning, Dad. How are you and Mom today?"

"Lillie's doing pretty good. We are about to have breakfast and get out of the house for a drive through the city later."

"That's wonderful, Dad," Olivia spoke softly.

"You know how much your mom loves driving around the community. We are planning to get out of the house for most of the day."

Her dad's voice was cheerful. The occasional outings in suburban Santa Cruz were a way to encourage Lillie's healing. Above everyone else, Edward was thankful for his wife's gradual return to days of love and intimacy between them.

"That's great. Dad, they found the plane." She said it quickly so he would not detect her panic. Her father's reaction was, for a moment, imprisoned by what his daughter said.

"Dad, are you there?"

"Yes, I heard you, Olivia. I wanted to ask if there was any word about it yesterday, but I was waiting for you to tell me. Right now, though, I want to know if you're okay. Are you okay, Honey?"

He wanted to show the strength of being the concerned father in Olivia's weak moment.

"I don't know... I just don't know. I'm afraid of... of what they're gonna' find."

Olivia prayed that a miracle would change what appeared to be a fateful outcome. She desperately wanted Eric to be alive but was also confounded and wanted answers. She would later call his parents to inform them of what she had just learned.

Officials had eventually located the wreckage scattered across one of Arizona's steepest mountains. The debris showed no obvious reasons for the crash, although experts speculated pilot error, combined with a series of mechanical malfunctions, as the cause of the accident. On one large piece of the charred wreckage tethered to a crushed gyroscopic turn coordinator, the words Klaus Industrial appeared on the clump of gnarled metal. Indications were that it would take the NTSB months of tedious work and careful investigation to reach satisfactory answers.

Rescue teams didn't find Eric at the scene and turned the focus on nearby slopes in search of him. One theory pointed to speculation that he perished when a part of the fuselage burst into flames on impact. Though possibly, he could be fighting to survive in a remote place where rescue teams had yet to search. The plane's Black Box, containing the most critical flight data had also been recovered.

All during the careful investigation, the NTSB dared life threatening conditions while sifting through snow covered wreckage on dangerously steep slopes. Until now, each piece of evidence led to a disappointing dead end. Tuesday marked a week since the crash. For Olivia, time was giving its way to a painful reality. Haunting memories of Eric infringed her and any hopes of his return were crushed. Seeking comfort, she penned a billet-doux from her heart to Eric.

Dear Eric,
Your absence is unbearably heartbreaking. Sleepless nights are tormenting, and not having answers to where you are, or fearing for your safety haunts me daily. I miss you and wish you were here with me. I miss your voice... your smile... your touch... I miss your love. My prayers for your safe return are unending. I love you, Erich every breath.
Forever yours, Olivia

Chapter 21
Returning?

Wednesday, 1:20 A.M. An unusually frigid winter had unexpectedly tapped on the doors in Southern California. The temperature dipped into the upper forties, and frosty conditions lingered over the valley, determined to leave a chilly mark on unsuspecting San Honestans. Rarely worn overcoats, their pockets hiding long-forgotten stray coins and crumpled receipts, came out of closets for a surprising spell of cold weather.

Days now, since the Cessna crashed, sleep hid from Olivia. Yet, for reasons unknown on this crisp wintery morning, she rested peacefully until the cell phone message beeps awakened her. Of late, every call before daylight brought with it heartbreaking news.

Cautiously, she checked her phone, trembling in a haze of fear and dread. The phone blinked a delayed voice text message that had been sent by Eric during the flight from New York which said, "Hello, Olivia I'm coming home to you."

Yet, except for a few people, no one knew that, while in Barcelona, Eric had mistakenly left the signed agreement made with Klaus Industrial in the Boardroom. So he returned to get it from the conference table. As he was about to enter the private meeting space, he heard familiar voices and stopped momentarily to ensure it was okay to proceed. It was then that he heard Hans instructing Boris to use whatever means to obtain the encryption data from Olivia.

Meanwhile, Eric decided not to confront Hans until he was back home, as the timeframe for returning to the Barcelona hotel, packing his belongings, and grabbing a quick nap was tight. Judging from what he'd heard, it was likely wise to keep quiet. He planned to inform Olivia that underhanded behavior was occurring. After the airport attack, authorities were made aware of what Eric knew, and Hans was placed under investigation secretly.

...And as it would turn out months later, Eric's fate on the Arizona mountains would be known.

The End